What Falls Away

For Scott
    Who's perserverd
and prospered. With
all best wishes for
your path ahead.

        Best,

        [signature]
        5/29/97
        Corvallis, OR

ALSO BY TRACY DAUGHERTY

The Woman in the Oil Field: Stories
Desire Provoked

Tracy Daugherty

What Falls Away

A NOVEL

W · W · Norton & Company · New York · London

T. S. Eliot, four lines from "The Rum Tum Tugger" from *Old Possum's Book of Practical Cats*. Copyright 1939 by T. S. Eliot and renewed © 1967 by Esme Valerie Eliot. Reprinted with the permission of Harcourt Brace & Company, Inc. and Faber & Faber Limited.

William Carlos Williams, six lines from "Rain" from *Collected Poems: 1909–1939, Volume 1*. Copyright 1939 by New Directions Publishing Corporation. Reprinted with the permission of the publisher.

The text of this book is composed in Bembo with the display set in Mistral.
Composition by PennSet, Inc.
Manufacturing by Courier Companies, Inc.
Book design by Jack Meserole

Library of Congress Cataloging-in-Publication Data
Daugherty, Tracy.
What falls away : a novel / Tracy Daugherty.
        p.   cm.
        I. Title.
        PS3554.A85W48   1996
        813'.54—dc20   95-21196

ISBN 0-393-03837-8

W. W. Norton & Company, Inc. 500 Fifth Avenue, New York, N.Y. 10110
W. W. Norton & Company Ltd., 10 Coptic Street, London WC1A 1PU

1 2 3 4 5 6 7 8 9 0

This book is the winner of the Associated Writing Programs Award for the Novel, 1994. AWP is a national nonprofit organization dedicated to serving American letters, writers, and programs of writing. AWP's headquarters are at George Mason University, Fairfax, Virginia.

For Grace: *Ayọdẹlẹ*

ACKNOWLEDGMENTS

Portions of this novel first appeared, in different form, in *Ontario Review* and *CutBank*, under the titles "Assailable Character" and "The Woman in the Oil Field," respectively. The author is grateful to the editors for permission to reprint.

Some of the background information (fictionalized herein) was suggested by Tad Bartimus and Scott McCartney in their book *Trinity's Children*.

My deepest thanks to Elizabeth Cox, Carol Houck Smith, Heather Schroder, Tracy Harris, D.W. Fenza, and the folks at the Associated Writing Programs.

I am grateful to the following people who read various early drafts of the novel and offered their advice: Elizabeth Campbell, Richard Daniels, Suzanne Gluck, Corrine Hales, Ehud Havazelet, Garrett Hongo, T.R. Hummer, Chang-rae Lee, Ted Leeson, George Manner, Inez Peterson, Maya Sonenberg, Teri Ruch, and Shelly Withrow.

Thanks also to the following people for their support: Marion Barthelme, Glenn Blake, Michelle Boisseau, Molly Brown, Rosellen Brown, Gene, JoAnne and Debra Daugherty, Olive Hershey, Edward Hirsch, David Landau, Phil and Frannie Levine, Ceci Miller-Kritsberg, Ann Mine, Jack Myers, Laura Rice, Gail Donohue Storey, Marshall Terry, and, most of all, Martha Grace Low.

Unworldly love
that has no hope
                    of the world

                    and that
cannot change the world
to its delight—

                    —WILLIAM CARLOS WILLIAMS

What falls away is always. And is near.

                    —THEODORE ROETHKE

One

THE MAN had parked his car on the limestone shoulder of the road, walked a few yards past caliche pits then two or three cactus stumps, and stood now in the clear half-moonlight in the middle of the dinosaur track. A business traveler of some kind, he wore olive slacks, a white shirt, and a fat green tie loosened at the collar. He had soft muscles (too much time behind a wheel), sagging breasts like pockets full of sand.

I watched him from the tiny window of my trailer home's kitchen. I'd been awake all night listening to the blasts. They didn't wake Peg and the kids anymore—or only sometimes, when the shaking was harder than usual. I was sitting at the table sipping instant coffee when I heard this fellow pull off the road.

He didn't look military or DOE. He didn't know the terrain, and seemed authentically shocked by the size of the track. The locals are used to dinosaur prints—fossils scar the whole Southwest—but no one I've met can tell me what sort of giant left this particular mark. In Arizona, Hopi or Navajo kids charge tourists a couple of bucks a shot to view tracks. When you ask them when the prints were made, the ones who've been to school will say "Jurassic" or "Pleistocene Epoch," but they're plucking wildly at memories of their textbooks. "Way long ago," a Hopi girl told me once. "Hundred years, like the moon."

Here in Nevada dinosaurs don't rate much. Everyone knows

there's more power in the desert at this very instant than Dino and his pals could ever have mustered.

But tonight this guy had apparently brushed the track with his brights and couldn't believe it. He stood now with his back to me, facing Sawmill Mountain and the Delamar Range. He knelt to place his palm in one of the toes, which formed a perfect crater in the rock. He'd need five or six hands to fill the space. Awed, he shook his head and laughed a little. He stood again, rubbed the back of his neck, and turned toward Vegas, a flat southerly glare blurring the hills. For a moment he cocked his head against the breeze as if he heard dimes spilling from a slot's silver mouth, and that's when the next blast came, the biggest of the night. My trailer shook. The windows hummed, the dirty knives in the sink jumped and beat each other. I heard Peg murmur in our bed. And the traveler, clearly just a salesman or a corporate foot soldier, an innocent on a lonely road heading somewhere he figured was important, stumbled to his car, panicked, uncertain—not the first man to come here late at night and be overwhelmed by something much larger than himself.

When Peg and the kids and I first arrived in Nevada we knew we'd found the end of the earth. This was hell—even to a man who was raised in West Texas and didn't blink twice at tumbleweeds, dust, and sun. My father had been a petroleum geologist in Midland, "as close to the ass end of the planet as I intend to get," he used to say. Aridity and level ground were all I ever knew as a boy, so I never complained. At night I rode my father's shoulders whenever he dumped the day's trash. We'd stand in the alley (rotten peaches at our feet, horned toads scurrying over pebbles, under old newspapers). He'd point out the Big Dipper but I never could see it. Meteors—and the spiky toads—frightened me. "It's good to be scared," he told me. "Teaches you caution, patience, awareness of others."

Cautiously, patiently, I grew up stunned at the sky's expanse and the world's flat face.

But in Nye County, Nevada, there isn't a solid face, or even much of a world. Just windblown wastes, midnight blasts, and ashy cones of light.

My father, retired, lives in Dallas now. We stopped to see him on our drive out west.

"*Where?*" he asked.

"Tilton," I told him. "Twenty miles east of the Nevada Test Site."

"What do they need an arts commissioner for?"

"They're keen on bringing culture to the desert," I said.

At that, my generally mild father, the only liberal oilman I've ever known, cursed the NRC, Westinghouse, General Electric: the entire nuclear industry. "Culture? What the hell do they know about culture? They're out to kill it!" he said.

Since his retirement and Ma's stroke, three years ago, he's become an active—and, I learned, curmudgeonly—supporter of the last of Texas's left-wing Democrats.

In his small suburban home he chooses to live now without the noise of television or radio. He gardens, works on his car—my son, with characteristic gracelessness, called his puttering "an old man's dance." His face is soft as a peach, his hands are big and worn.

We stayed with him for five days. In all that time he took us on a single sight-seeing tour: the old schoolbook depository overlooking Dealey Plaza. My kids had only seen pictures of it. For Dad it's forever a tragic shrine.

"The country'll never recover from Oswald's rifle in the window," he said the day we went. We'd followed a guide up several flights of stairs inside the building. Dad started to cry. He told Scott and Dana he pitied them for the second-rate nation they'd inherited from Nixon and Reagan. If Kennedy had lived, he argued—I'd heard this all my life—we'd never have had Vietnam, we'd have established an equitable economy, we'd have ended the nuclear arms race.

"That'd be great, Gramps," Dana said. Scott, bored, made faces at the floor. Dad frowned at my daughter. "What grades are you in now?" he asked.

"Fourth," she said. "Scott's a freshman in high school."

"Well, you're old enough to know your country's history then." He pointed from the famous sixth-floor window. "Look over there. On the skyscraper. See that horse?" We followed his finger, but all we saw was a thicket of glass and steel. "Of course you can't," Dad said. "These cheap modern buildings have smothered it." If they weren't there, he told us, we'd see a revolving red Pegasus, rearing and about to take flight. "It's a beautiful sign," Dad said. "The Mobil Oil Company raised it years ago. The state protects it now. It's a hidden Texas landmark." He stood on his toes, as if *he'd* decided to fly.

He said he was sad that few people today know the company whose trademark the horse had been, and fewer still can recite the legend of Pegasus. I'd never heard him like this: weepy, drifting.

"So many losses," he went on. My kids were cold and ready to go. They couldn't wait to see the sequined showgirls Peg had promised them in Vegas. "Like Jack Ruby's bar," Dad said. "Can anyone find its old spot? A few tourists pose for photos in front of the plaza, but that's all. No one talks about it much. No one talks about the sky we can't see behind the streetlights." He squeezed my arm. "Remember, Jon? Do you?" It hurt me to hear him so scattered. "Remember the sky out west?"

"Sure," I said. I patted his hand.

"The Milky Way was as bright as lightning. The air—hell, the whole damned country, it seemed—crackled with promise then. Camelot! And your mother was in fine shape." He laughed, then shook his head. "Jon, Jon."

"What is it, Dad?"

He glanced at my kids. "Us," he said. His gaze shifted to the streets. His lips trembled. "All of us."

He aged five years right then; or maybe I *saw* his age for the first time that visit.

"We've forgotten falling stars," he said, "and all the things that used to scare us."

That same afternoon, he took me to the Parkview Manor Retirement Home to see my mother. She's seventy-eight years old. Lately she's been hallucinating a woman in her room—a prostitute, an "oil field gal" she claims my father had a fling with when he was a young roughneck living on rigs. Dad says he's never had an affair in his life, and I believe him.

When we entered Mother's room that day she began screaming at him. He sat patiently by her bed. "She teases me," she told him. "That old oil field woman. She comes to me at night and tells me I won't ever sleep with you again. Then she ties my bed to a gelding and he runs me around a pasture, fast and dizzy, and the whole time she's laughing. In the mornings when the women here bathe me she's outside my window and I try to hide my body but they won't let me. They want to show her what I've become. Do you want her to laugh at me? Am I repulsive to you now?"

She's had a long, varied life, but it all boils down to this: a misplaced jealousy she's held for sixty years.

I didn't know what to say to her. I wasn't sure she even knew I was there. Dad had seen her this way several times and no longer minded her accusations. He leaned over, kissed her forehead, and whispered, "Sweet dreams, baby."

Each night after that, from hundreds of miles away, I wished them *both* sweet dreams. It's all I knew to do for them.

I-20 West, through Dallas, Fort Worth, Abilene, Big Spring, Midland-Odessa, runs past refineries and rigs and, through its tributaries, all the way to Vegas. Flames breathe fiercely out of steel-plated towers and drums; the air smells flat, like warm asparagus.

When I was my daughter's age I wanted to ride the oil pumps in West Texas's fields. They bucked up and down like the wild-maned rodeo broncos I saw on TV, or like coin-operated horses in front of the dime stores Mama used to shop.

The day we left Dallas, thick blue thunderheads rose in the east. A faint smell of rain mingled with sand in the air. We stopped in Abilene for onion rings. The Dairy Queen was overrun with high school majorettes. They wore green-and-yellow uniforms and hats with plumes. Big, strapping Texas girls: I was reminded of old Kodaks I'd seen of my mother when she was a junior high pep rally queen.

All the way to Nevada I mentally fought the possibility that I might not see my folks again. Mama didn't know her dreams from the world; Dad's frailty had startled me. I kept picturing him in the book depository, crouched like Oswald in failing, musty light, shaking and crying.

My parents were beyond any comfort my love could give them now. Dad refused my offers of extra money, extra time with him. "You've got your own life now," he said. "Don't worry about us."

Concentrate on Peg and the kids, I thought—so far, you haven't offered them much of a bargain. Here I was, uprooting them for the fourth time in six years. No permanent home. No lasting friendships. "When cities hit hard times, art's the first fat we trim," Houston's mayor once told me. Texas; Portland, Oregon; Moscow, Idaho. My family had gotten used to the road.

Now tumbleweeds were blowing across the interstate. I couldn't tell the towns of West Texas apart anymore since the damn franchises had moved in everywhere. Burger Kings and Motel Sixes. HBO and Showtime blaring in people's houses, through the windows.

That first night out of Dallas we stopped at a cinder-block motel—the Rayola—in Monahans. A rusty sign above the office door showed a cowboy in pajamas and a nightcap sitting up in bed, still wearing his boots, twirling a lariat.

After check-in, Dana and Scott walked across the highway to a pizza place. Peg and I were too bushed to eat. We talked some more about my job. Maybe this is it, she said, a chance to settle —though Tilton, Nevada, home of a large military base, was hardly Shangri-la. Why the town wanted me—a financier for theater, opera, ballet—was still a mystery. It didn't even have an amateur playhouse. But I was promised a decent salary, security, and a changing, more favorable climate for the arts.

My job interview two months back had been conducted by an army general and a representative from the Reynolds Electrical and Engineering Company. The town didn't seem to have a civic council or an arts committee.

When Peg and the kids hit the sack I sat smoking, staring at David Letterman and the tan brick wall of our room. I thought again of my mother's sad hallucinations, my father's grief. All day I'd been holding back tears of loss. Now they finally came. After a few shaky minutes I felt better, relieved of a burden.

I lighted a second cigarette, dropped ashes into a motel glass. It was wrapped in clear plastic when I first picked it up, but now I noticed a lipstick stain on its rim. A ghostly kiss. I lay awake, listening to rain wash the streets and tap the curtained window.

2

WEST OF ODESSA there used to be a meteor crater. I remember seeing it as a kid: a rock bowl, perfectly smooth, carved deep into the planet. Now it's filled nearly to the lip with dirt and old hamburger wrappers. The oil boom's over in that part of Texas—the parks are overgrown, the rigs are left standing just for show. Ghost towns. Most of the fields are depleted. If you pump oil out of the earth too fast, my father told me once, the salt domes under the soil will collapse, and sinkholes open in the land, spreading through weeded lots, rippling under farm roads, shattering concrete. In the past whole communities have disappeared, he said. Swing sets, dress shops, signs.

Roswell, New Mexico. We slowed for a Texaco station; semis swished by us, kicking up gravel and dust. The traffic made Scott nervous.

As soon as I stopped the car he bolted out the door. He paced quickly in a circle around the gas pumps and shouted, "Fuck! Shit! Fuck! Shit!"

Peg was the first to reach him. She ran up behind him and clamped her arms around his chest, pinning his hands to his ribs —her usual way of soothing him.

My son was born wrong. *He* puts it that way; Peg and I have never judged him or qualified our love. He suffers severe depressions, bouts of wild rage so volcanic and consuming he doesn't remember them later. He broods on my every word; an offhand remark—like "Congress is out of control"—can keep him up all night. He'll sit obsessively in front of the television, howling at the senators on C-Span.

Last year he had a bad reaction—or maybe *no* reaction—to Prozac. Whatever the reason, he was suicidal all summer, and Peg and I never left his side. We still hover; we can't help it. Dana feels neglected much of the time. Before she lost Bernie, a cotton panda Peg made for her when she was a baby, she'd cope by hugging the stuffing out of him.

That day in Roswell, while her mother wrestled with Scott near the diesel pumps, she pretended not to care. She searched her purse for change, then bought herself a candy bar.

I stood back while Peg worked on Scott. In a car dealership connected to the gas lot, a man sold a young couple a used Toyota. The ripped screens of an old drive-in theater, closed for years, floated over the highway like cloudbanks on the horizon.

Scott was laughing now through tears. Peg held his arm. I imagined actors' faces on the movie screens, their mouths as wide as tractors, kissing, singing. Delirious with joy. I tried to picture Peg and myself and the kids up there, holding hands and dancing. "I'm sorry," Scott said. His face was pink. "I don't know what happened. I just all of a sudden—"

"It's all right, kiddo," Peg said. She stroked the car's hood. "I'm going stir-crazy myself. You want a Coke or something?"

"Yeah."

She gave him a handful of coins, and he wandered off toward the battered red soft drink machine.

I glanced at Peg. She shrugged. "We need to get there soon," she said. "We need to establish a nice, easy routine. We need to start our lives."

Jets hurtled across the sky, into or out of a nearby air force base. The day rumbled with sun-warmed metal. For a moment, as I gripped Peg's hands, I wanted to free myself like a hawk, like a flying horse, from the ground's heavy pull.

In eastern Arizona we came to a town whose population was entirely Japanese-American. By the "Welcome to Our City" sign, two young girls in blazing blue kimonos—cheap costumes designed to draw tourists—sat in the sand selling rice cakes, corsages, rubber balls, confections they called *manju,* and vinegared rice dolls. Dana wanted a doll, so we stopped. Scott bought a ball, which he later tossed against the windshield as I drove, annoying the hell out of me.

The girls explained that their grandfathers had been kept in a relocation camp here during the Second World War. When the war ended and the army left this area, several Japanese-American families remained to raise cattle. In time a town flourished.

At the mention of war, Scott began to shout at a long purple mesa on the horizon. Peg couldn't calm him at first. His agony cost us a good two hours and scared the wits out of the poor young girls.

At that point I would've traded the job, this trip, my whole damn career for a son I could talk to without fear of planting a nightmare in his mind.

Later that day, when we crossed the border into Nevada near Lake Mead and the muddy Virgin River, the air thickened with humidity and the earth, full of copper, turned red. At the time I couldn't explain it but I felt claustrophobic in all this open space. Now I know none of the water that streams into the desert ever gets out. The rivers empty into lakes, drain into natural sinks, or simply leak away and evaporate. Somehow that first day I sensed the maddening circularity of life here.

We were eager to see our home, so the kids agreed to just a peek at Vegas. Peg promised we'd come back and catch a show after we'd settled in Tilton. On our pass through town we glimpsed the Shoot-Out Club, the Pioneer Casino, the Railway

Lounge—names which suggested a frontier adventure, but only for the reckless and the brave.

Red neon cast various shades of anger, arousal, embarrassment into the streets.

We stopped at a Burger King, then headed north to Tilton. Sagebrush, deserted mine shafts, and peeling billboards littered the hills. Scott was impressed that we could pull over anywhere for an open-air piss. There wasn't another car within a hundred miles of us on this road, so no one would see us. I began to look for buzzards—and found them, on sandy rocks, in the air.

As the evening shadows moved, the cliff walls on either side of the highway reminded me of the peasants' chiseled faces in Orozco's or Rivera's magnificent murals: large, serious heads gazing in sorrow at the world.

Fifty miles from Tilton we noticed a series of "ranches"— Nevadan for legalized prostitution inns. Signs flashed MASSAGE MASSAGE MASSAGE in the night, and "Servicemen Especially Welcome/Good Job in the Gulf."

"Great," Peg said. "It's like a theme park. Welcome to Sperm World."

On the outskirts of Tilton, in a sagebrush-lined city park glowing with sodium lights, kids climbed monkey bars, slides, and small-scale replicas of Pershing missiles, painted like Christmas-tree ornaments.

At the edge of the park a grizzled man in a sweater and a plastic raincoat crouched above a small fire. The night was sweltering, dry. The kids on the playground ignored him, as though he were a dead shrub.

In the dark we couldn't tell much about the town. The Tilton Chamber of Commerce had sent us a real estate brochure and some classified ads, but we hadn't committed to anything. We wanted to look around first.

We checked into a Best Western, and I phoned the general who'd interviewed me. He welcomed me to town. He said a colleague of his would meet me for lunch tomorrow at the Atomic Diner on Main Street. I still had no idea who I'd be working with—or where. The general had seemed forthcoming when we met, generous and loud, but I hadn't probed him enough. In our excitement, Peg and I hadn't thought much about details. Work had been hard to find. We were grateful for anything.

Before going to bed that first night I thumbed through the phone book. Military titles appeared with most names. There weren't many civilians in Tilton.

At noon the following day I met Major Donaldson at the Atomic Diner. The tables and booths were a faded sherbet color. Framed pictures of Cruise, MX, and Trident I missiles, along with an autographed photo of Jack Dempsey, lined the wall behind the cracked Formica counter. Summer horseflies buzzed steaming pots of chili.

Major Donaldson gripped my hand. "Call me Lynn," he said. "People used to kid me about my name, but I got no problem with it. You got a problem with it?"

"No," I said.

"Good." We sat. He tapped a silver medal on his uniform. "101st Airborne," he said. " 'Sixty-nine to '70. General Thompson tells me you've never been a grunt."

"That's right."

"Too bad. Missed a good show. Now then, Mr. Chase, we've got your living arrangements all squared away—"

"You have?"

"Two-story Colonial job. Beautiful work. Of course, we took into account your salary range."

"My wife and I were hoping to study the market—"

"Best leave everything to us." When he smiled, his cheeks were brassy knobs. "We know the lay of the land. So, as I say, everything's set, but it's not quite ready yet. Plumbing fixtures, wiring—we'll take care of them."

I said, "Who's 'we'?"

"All of us. The town." The waiter arrived. Lynn told him, "I'll have the Fallout Burger and some of those Afterburner Fries." I thought he was kidding until I looked at the menu. He winked at me. "Can't beat it." I ordered the same. "In the meantime we got you a nice trailer home west of here a couple of miles. I don't imagine you'll be there more'n a month."

He told me Tilton's residents were delighted to have me on board. "We took a poll last year, asked everyone in town what we needed to make a better community. Everyone answered more or less the same. Plays, musicals, museums, those sorts of things. Now, I'm not much of an opera man myself, and I never liked stage shows much, though I go for a good strip-tease when it's done with taste." He nudged my arm. "But we all know the arts are good for us. It's sort of a spiritual need we've been missing. Feed the soul, right? Jump-start our hearts and minds. We're thrilled to have you here. I mean it."

I didn't know whether to laugh or cringe. He wasn't faking this Yahoo bit. He was a born-and-bred natural.

"Actually, just between you and me . . ." He lowered his voice. "I liked that movie *Patton*. With what's-his-name? I thought I could do what he did. The way he grabbed your attention, you know? His presence. I think there's a little bit of an actor in every military man."

"You may be right," I said.

"So, let's say, if you were to do a local production—"

"Would you like to try out for a part?"

He grinned. "When this all came up—about whether or not to hire an arts guy—a lot of my colleagues weren't sure. But I thought it was a great idea, right from the start."

He said temporary office space would be provided for me downtown until a permanent arts facility could be built. The contractors were hoping for my design input, but of course my security clearance would have to go through first. When I asked, "What security clearance?" he said, "The general didn't tell you? Anytime you work in a military community, Mr. Chase, you've got to be checked out, top to bottom. Friends, family, professional and private affiliations—"

I laughed. "You think I'm a spy?"

He didn't smile. "It'll take about a year for full clearance, but don't worry. You'll receive a regular paycheck each month . . . we're proceeding on the assumption that everything's fine."

"And if I don't pass your test?"

"You have anything to hide?"

As part of an artists' tour I'd flown to Nicaragua in '86, when the United States was funding the contra rebels in their war with the Sandinistas, but I'd listed that clearly on my résumé under "International Arts Exchanges." Surely Lynn would have said something if the trip had been a problem. "No," I said. "But—"

"It's just a formality, Jon. May I call you Jon? Ah, here we go. These fries'll knock your belly clear back into the next booth." He leaned forward and whispered, "The secret's a well-gauged combo of vinegar and cayenne pepper."

I didn't know what to tell him, or what to say about the "town's" plans for us. The spicy food made my eyes water. Lynn greeted several friends. "You're going to like it here, Jon," he told me. "Nice folks, good place to raise your kids. My colleagues here are thoroughly professional—not like *some* of the gigs I've been assigned to." He sprinkled his fries with Tabasco. "Back in '75 I was at Travis Air Force Base—Sacramento—loading nuclear missiles onto B-52s. Routine procedure night after night. One evening I check out early. When I get home the goddam phone's ringing. Coded message: get back to base. I'm thinking, 'Shithouse mouse.' Top security, everyone in a panic. Turns out, this one bright boy pulled the wrong handle on a plane and spilled two missiles. Decoys, thank God, but one of 'em's crushed the other, and jet fuel—hundreds of gallons of it—is leaking all over, around twenty primed birds. One little spark and Sacramento's a memory, know what I mean?"

"I know what you mean."

"Dumb fuckin' shits—"

"Lynn, listen," I said. I wiped my eyes. "About the house—"

"Don't mention it. We're glad to help."

"I'd like some choice here," I said. "A home is a very personal matter. My wife and I may prefer another neighborhood than the one you've picked for us. I mean, I'm not questioning your taste or intentions or anything—but, you know, we'll have to look at school districts—"

"Jon." He folded his hands on the table. "Couple of things you've got to understand right off the bat. Tilton's not your average little community."

"I've noticed."

"We're proud of the work we do here, but it has its risks, and everyone has to observe certain protocols."

"I'm not in the army, Lynn."

"Not technically, no, but—" With his chin he pointed out the window, toward a housing development beneath a twisted hill. Three young boys were kicking a soccer ball against the slope. "Several years ago those families—civilian engineers, mostly—chose to ignore our warnings and went ahead and built there."

The homes were spacious and clean, with rock gardens rather than lawns. Barring a massive earthquake, there didn't seem to be any avalanche danger.

"See the indented part of the hill?" Lynn said. "That reddish dirt area right above where the boys are kicking their ball?"

I noticed a series of concave impressions in the ground.

"Because of the soil's density there—or rather its *absorbency*—it's a prime spot for burying waste."

"What are you getting at?"

"Well, often after certain tests, various residues remain—"

"Wait a minute," I said. "Are you telling me those kids are playing in radioactive waste?" I laughed nervously.

Lynn closed his eyes for a moment. "I can neither confirm

nor deny the presence of hot material in that area," he said. "But I strongly urge you to leave your housing to us."

Peg paced the motel room. "Right. I suppose they'll also pick out our shower curtains, our upholstery, the size of our welcome mat," she said. "Kitchen wallpaper with a nice machine-gun motif. Jesus, Jon. A bunch of paratroopers are going to call the shots on our interior design?"

"I know, I know," I said. I threw my shaving kit into my suitcase. "We're out of here. It's a nightmare."

"Absolutely." She folded a pair of Dana's jeans, then stopped and rubbed her face. "We can't do this," she said quietly through her hands.

"What can't we do?"

"Leave. It's the only thing we've got right now."

"Anything's better than this. We'll find something."

She shook her head. "Remember last year? Last fall? When Scott needed medicine and there was no insurance to cover it? I can't go through that again, Jon. *Scott* can't."

"The place is poisoned, Peg."

"Surely they know what they're doing," she said. "I mean, they get paid to know what they're doing, right?"

"You don't really believe that."

"I don't know. Not really. But I don't think we have any choice. Not until we locate something else. Have it in hand."

The exhaustion in her voice took the starch out of me. I shut my suitcase.

She tried to smile. "Other families live here, right?"

I pulled her onto the bed with me and kissed her neck. "I suppose they do." I plucked a barrette from her hair. The kids were out swimming in the pool. "You know what occurs to me? We're alone here," I told her. "When's the last time *that* happened?"

"I never thought I'd be drafted into the army," she said, squeezing my wrist. I loosened her belt.

In how many beds in how many places had we made love? The swell of her breasts in my hands, the thimble of her navel, were my only constants in a life of domestic change.

I locked the door and drew the blinds. She closed her eyes. "I'm so tired," she said.

"I know." I slipped her cotton blouse past her shoulders, slid my hand beneath her skirt. "I don't care where we live," I whispered. "I just want you with me. I love you so much, Peg. Peggy."

She massaged my neck. I turned her over gently, kissed and licked her belly until her hips began to move against my arms. I removed her skirt and panties, spread her thighs, then stroked her with my lips and tongue.

Her abdomen rippled. "*You're* my home," I whispered. I nestled kisses into the soft spaces where her legs met her sex. She tasted of salt. Her smell was the newborn damp of Scott and Dana. I rubbed my face in her skin. She said my name, gripped my hair. "Here," I said. "Here's where I live." Her back arched and she quietly cried, spoke her love for me, escaped the room, Nevada, the searing sunlight through gaps in the blinds, everything but the bright, breaking wave of her own warm pleasure.

The best home we ever lived in was a renovated farmhouse in the foothills of the Coast Range Mountains south of Portland, Oregon. Scott was only five then; his depression hadn't yet burst through his skin. I had just been hired as a community services coordinator for the Oregon Arts Commission. Peg and I were certain we'd spend the rest of our lives in the Northwest.

The house itself, a rental, wasn't spectacular—it was too small—but the location was ideal: forty miles from the ocean. Scott loved the Pacific Coast, the winding wet road between Waldport and Newport, then down to the caves where the speckled seals barked and slept and swam. When I picture my son happy, I see him in that long-ago landscape. We'd picnic in the woods above the salty cliffs—stark cypresses stiff against the wind.

White pines shook starburst needles in our eyes, jays cackled at our meager cheese sandwiches, smashed in the bag when Scott, jumping with excitement, sat on them in the car. Below us, mussels clumped on rocks opened their crusty mouths to the sun; the tide, gathering strength, spread its quiet confusion among silt-and-crab-and-rock deposits, leaving pebbles and foam; wherever it touched, ruddy brown plankton sucked the shifting earth, the white hollow wood on the beach. Each time, as we ate, I'd feel a kind of giddy joy, a pleasure in the teeming buzz all about us. On the coast I always felt I'd landed on solid ground again, after weeks of abstract work, and the rustling life I heard around me was like the colorful silk of my parachute snapping in the wind, falling, about to engulf me as I untangled myself from recent days' clinging, bothersome strings. . . .

Peg seemed pleasantly dizzy too back then, with heat and scents and the *click click* of Scott's plastic shovel on a lichen-smothered log.

She's convinced Scott's problems began after my position was cut and we were forced to go to Idaho, then back to Texas, spending most of our time in cities, away from water and trees. But I don't remember things that way. Cities had their pleasures too, which Scott seemed to enjoy. In Houston he and I loved the Chinese market, bursting with arrogant, salty food smells in the shade of a freeway. Fish cakes, cabbage, *Kal-Pis* in coolers, chili oil, plum sauce. Oysters. With garrulous delight, the merchants plunged their hands into bags of raw pork, bean threads, sesame seeds. Everywhere we looked, we were blessed with variety, color, and choice.

I don't know when I first noticed Scott's troubles. At one point he stopped going to the market with me. That should've been a sign. By then, I suppose, I was too worried about home ownership and insurance policies to see his gradual change. We had a starter house in Houston. Dana had been born. I imagined buying and selling homes for a few years until we had enough credit to move into the big leagues—the fancy neighborhoods like River Oaks. But the graph of my career is hardly a straight line up.

I celebrated my forty-fourth birthday in a government-owned trailer house on the edge of the Nevada Test Site.

Why did we stay, when all the early indications spelled disaster? Dwindling savings, exhaustion from the road . . . looking back, I see that Peg was right: we *needed* to stay. Besides that, I got no nibbles from the job queries I mailed out each week.

Peg baked a chocolate cake for me—it was our first Saturday in Tilton. The kids gave me goofy wind-up toys: plastic animals that danced, flipped, or smacked drums. They were jokes—a few nights earlier we'd visited our immediate neighbors; their homes were full of cheap little do-dads like these. Three other trailers formed a ragged row with ours. The town had promised all three families permanent housing, but they'd waited for over a year. One of the men was an electrical engineer, the other two were technicians. I was tired the night we met, so they didn't make much of an impression on me. What I *did* remember later was shelves of tiny porcelain owls, candles shaped like clowns, brass frog bookends, wind-up toys. The engineer's wife caught me staring at her miniature velvet paintings (earth-toned portraits of Hemingway, Christ, Don Quixote). "Aren't those cute?" she said. "I got them at the five and ten downtown. They have the most wonderful decorator items there."

She wore spiky steel hair curlers and fuzzy house shoes: a TV sitcom wife.

As we walked back home the kids giggled. I hummed the old *Twilight Zone* theme.

"Night of the Living Knickknacks," said Peg.

I said, "Bad Taste, U.S.A."

"Are we being snobbish?"

"Of course. Let's enjoy it."

After I'd blown out my birthday candles, Scott and Dana went outside to play in the dinosaur track. I was grateful to them—

privacy was hard to come by in the trailer. Except for a bathroom and a kitchen, it was one big space.

We tossed Bernie, Dana's panda, onto the floor and snuggled together on our springy fold-out couch. We kissed, but the cramped quarters, our awareness of all that needed to be done, and the sound of our kids' voices outside distracted us from each other. As always, Scott was our biggest problem. We didn't know whether to send him to a public or a private school, or hire a tutor for him here at home. In the past we'd tried all three, with varying results. He'd seemed better since we'd arrived, less angry and stressed than he'd been on the road. I suggested we go ahead and try Tilton High—alert Scott's teachers to his instabilities and have them monitor him closely. Peg tentatively agreed.

My job started in two days. No one had told me what kind of budget I had to work with, how much staff I could hire, what my priorities should be.

"Maybe I'll start with you," I told Peg. "A one-woman show. What do you say?"

"I don't think Tilton, Nevada, is ready for me."

Peg's a first-rate dancer—we first met at a party after one of her shows in Santa Fe. A classically trained ballerina, she does performance art now, like the "happenings" of the sixties, only far more challenging and intelligent. (In part she's changed her style, because as she's moved into her thirties she's lost some flexibility in her ankles.)

Her newest principle is "Order is arbitrary." Dance should be freed from narrative and plot. Spontaneity's truer to life.

I was determined to work her into Tilton's first season of shows. I imagined posters of her face brightening grocery stores, diners, banks—her short black bangs, her lovely smile. The town needed a shot of beauty, a burst of creative energy. It needed variety, color, choice. It needed to wake up.

3

THE FIRST TIME we heard a missile test we all woke screaming in the night. Scott hid beneath his sheet. Dana clung to Bernie; she thought a bogeyman had come to get her. He was lurking outside, rattling the trailer.

Peg, groggy, thought the gas stove had blown. I wondered if we'd had an earthquake, a meteor strike, a sinkhole eruption . . .

Horned toads in the alley. Oswald's rifle.

All the things that used to scare us.

The following morning, early, I was banging on Lynn's door. He lived downtown. He greeted me wearing boxer shorts and a T-shirt. In the morning light the muscles in his neck gleamed like ripples in a wet suit.

His living room was nearly empty. A couch-bed, a small desk, a black-and-white Zenith TV. An open bottle of Wild Turkey sat on the light green carpet.

I asked him about last night's explosions.

"Routine," he said. He yawned. "Come on in."

I was confused. Just yesterday I'd read in the paper that since the breakup of the former Soviet Union no new missiles had been built in the United States.

When I mentioned this, Lynn admitted, "Weapons production hasn't stopped altogether here, but it *has* been severely curtailed. You can keep a secret, can't you, Jon?" He smiled at me.

Every twelve days or so, he said, the army and the Department of Energy still conducted underground detonation surveys at the Test Site. "Only six tests a year are nuclear, but we need to stay in practice. The Cold War may have ended, but we have to keep our guard up for any impending situations."

"This wasn't underground," I told him. "This was up above. The whole trailer shook."

"Uh-uh," Lynn said. "Limited Test Ban Treaty, 1963. We agreed with the Soviets to suspend all atmospheric testing." He grinned. " 'Course, those Roosky mothers aren't around anymore, are they?"

"I swear this blast came from the sky," I said.

"No way. The whole world'd jump down our throats. Besides, since the early days we don't leak hot stuff into the air."

I didn't believe him—I knew what I'd heard (the blasts sounded like the shells I'd heard falling years ago in the hills of Nicaragua, only louder)—but short of quitting a job I'd barely begun and stranding my family again, I didn't know how to react.

Lynn picked up the Wild Turkey bottle and set it in a corner next to a curved machete with a gold handle. "You like that? That's a kukri," he said, watching my eyes. "Sharp side's on the left. You swing it like this." He unsheathed the blade, held the kukri in his right hand, and chopped the air with a backstroke. "Nifty little item I picked up in Southeast Asia. It's fun at parties." He set the machete back down. "You're just in time for breakfast, Jon." He walked into his kitchen and pulled a small round bundle out of a pantry. "British ratpack. You want one?"

"No thanks."

"You sure? New town, new job—you'll need your morning pep. Used to be, the going rate in NATO was two American C-rats for one of these." He opened the cloth kit: chicken, instant coffee, milk paste in a tube, a Mars bar, a block of dried oatmeal. "I got hooked on 'em a few years ago when I did some demolition work with the Brits. Remember the Falklands? Major realignment of the landscape. . . ."

On Lynn's TV, a morning sports show played home-run highlights from last night's Astros-Padres game. Baseball season was nearly over; football was well underway. "Those suckers can't hit their way out of a paper bag," Lynn said, watching the screen, munching his chicken. "Who d'you think's gonna win the pennant this year?"

I shook my head. He saw I was still concerned about the blasts. "Look, rest easy, Jon." He set his breakfast down. "Missile tests are very simple things, okay? You want to know how they work? I'll tell you how they work. Maybe that'll settle your mind, huh?"

"What if I'm a spy?" I said.

He laughed. "It's no big deal, really, nothing to worry about. Ask anyone. Anyone in town. Here's the whole story, nutshell. First you put your warhead in a canister, right? Insert the canister into a vertical shaft a thousand feet or so in the ground, then fill the shaft with epoxy and gravel to absorb the radiation." He clapped his hands. "Neat and clean. No danger to anyone."

He said proudly, "The Apollo astronauts used to train for their moonwalks here, we've got so many craters."

Later at home, Peg and I talked again about leaving, trusting that something would open up, but neither of us saw much choice. More than a steady income, we needed stability, routine —not just for Scott, but for all of us. I wrote to every gallery, community theater, and museum I knew in every major city in the country, but they all informed me this was a "bad time" for the arts.

In the following weeks I read everything I could find about the Test Site, from army pamphlets to Nevada history books. The Site itself, the restricted area, I learned, is about the size of Rhode Island. The Department of Energy began nuclear weapons testing here in 1951; to date, the government acknowledges "approximately" nine hundred nuclear explosions in the vicinity. Over one hundred of these blasts were not announced publicly, but were discovered later by independent seismologists. No one knows how many tests have actually been made.

From '51 to '62, over 120 bombs thundered in the air. Midnight fireballs brought instant daylight to Reno, three hundred miles to the west. Elaborate, life-size "doom towns" were erected in the desert to test the bombs' effects on houses and buildings. Routinely, soldiers were posted within the radiation zone so their symptoms could later be studied.

Today the DOE claims to have perfected its safety procedures and to have stopped exposing people to danger. The government admits, however, that the Test Site is a waste dump for thorium, and that Yucca Mountain, west of here, is targeted to be the central repository for America's nuclear leftovers.

My father, recalling his geology, told me on the phone that thirty-two known fault lines split Yucca Mountain.

"All right, the first thing we do is buy bottled water each week," I told Peg once I'd absorbed all these facts. "God knows what the aquifer looks like here. I don't want us drinking from the tap, not even when we brush our teeth, okay? The kids are not allowed to wander out of sight when they play. And in town, if we get lost, we don't just bop around. Ask for help. Don't go anywhere you're not assured is safe—and even then, trust your instincts."

At night I'd gaze at the moonlit land. It seemed an endless extension of that little West Texas alley where my father left our trash, the bags of boxes and grease and soap-stiffened wafers of hair from the tub. The family odors that once were disgusting (old meat, wilted drippy lettuce, dirty balls of cotton and wadded tissues) filled me now, in memory, with longing—for what I wasn't sure. A simpler time?

Meteors burned each night like streaking red horses in the sky.

MY TEST SITE LESSONS were enhanced by several old cattle ranchers—men my father's age—I met in the diner or at the post office, my first three months in Tilton. They told me how the government acquired acreage in Nevada, New Mexico, Wyoming, and Colorado that's now its nuclear heart. During the Second World War, they said, the army rolled out west and convinced ranchers that their land was needed for weapons R&D, otherwise the war was lost. Families left their homes, sold their animals. They believed everything would be returned to them once the war was over. Sometimes men were granted hunting privileges on land that had once been theirs (unaware that they were exposing themselves to radiation).

Once, the Milky Way had swept the brightest arm across the sky; now searchlights roamed the stars, guiding cargo planes toward not-so-secret landing strips.

As I listened to these old men talk I understood the longing I'd lately felt. I wanted the faith my father once had in our nation. His generation evolved in a fanfare of trust. The GIs won the war with Germany and Japan. They returned from Europe, bought new homes, invested in stocks. Uncle Sam pledged to keep them safe. Disappointment only came later, once their trust had fossilized into clear belief.

My generation, raised on advertising's lurid charms, empty presidential visions, the Kennedy and King assassinations, the swamps of Vietnam, Watergate, Chernobyl, has been warped by the certainty of betrayal.

At night, as I felt the ground let go beneath my sleeping kids, I knew faith was not an option for me.

Eventually, my friends told me what I'd already guessed: after the Japanese surrendered, the army kept the land it had grabbed. At first, military spokesmen said there were safety concerns. True enough. The ranchers' houses, barns, and fields had been hopelessly contaminated. Bleached-white deer lay dead for miles in several counties. Plutonium rode deep into the desert on the backs of stinging dust storms.

Trinitite, a marblelike glass formed when the heat of a blast melts sand, became a valued prize among ranchers' kids, until the radiation danger was at least partly understood.

In time the families who'd lost their homes realized they'd never get them back. Faced with a "rising Communist menace," the army insisted it was forced to develop new weapons. The searchlights, the rumbling, the stenches in the air, the explosions persisted, all in the holy name of national security.

The Second World War was still being fought here.

My office was plywood and corrugated tin—about the size of a bus. It was attached to a former gymnasium the town planned to convert into an arts arena. One wall wasn't finished; plastic sheeting, sacks of cement, and buckets of grout blocked the filing cabinets. The wooden desk was roundly scarred, as though someone in a rage had beaten it with a hammer.

My first morning, Lynn introduced me to a young man named Chick, one of the few civilians I'd seen. He'd be my administrative assistant. He was bent, thin, and slightly green around the ears, like a sun-bleached saguaro. He didn't seem real to me—excessively soft or something, like an inflatable toy.

"You know anything about the arts, Chick?" I asked him once Lynn had left.

"No." He hugged an empty clipboard to his chest.

I watched sand batter the plastic sheeting. Nine in the morning and the day was lost already to heat, wind, rising torpor. "What about fund-raising?"

"No sir."

"Don't ever call me 'sir.' This isn't the goddam army. How did you get this job?"

"My father's a friend of—"

"Right. We're just one happy family here in Tilton, aren't we?"

"Excuse me?"

"Okay, Chick, Major Donaldson may have stuck me with you, but just remember I didn't call the hire—I wasn't even consulted about it." I was too hard on him, I knew—my anger wasn't as great as I made it seem—but I couldn't let Lynn run me over before I'd even gotten started. I had to plant my feet. "I don't know if I have the power to fire you, but I surely have the means to make your life a living hell if you screw up, understand?"

"Yes sir."

I slammed my hand on the desk. "Don't call me 'sir'!"

Chick confirmed that Tilton was 100 percent culture-dead. For edification and entertainment, men drank in bars or in the bowling alley. Women read magazines in the beauty parlor, kids watched television at home. High schoolers circled the Atomic Diner's parking lot late at night in their cars, looking for action.

My budget was a handful of spit, and it was going to be difficult to raise funds in the middle of nowhere. I figured a film series would be the easiest program to get off the ground. A projector wouldn't cost much, and old movies rented cheaply.

We could start with *Dr. Strangelove*.

The gym next door was too small for even a regulation basketball court, much less a stage, seating, dressing rooms, audio equipment, etc. "This won't do at all," I said. "Does the high school have an auditorium?"

"Just a gym, about this size," Chick said. "There's the football stadium—"

"Jesus Christ. Call Lynn."

"We don't have a phone yet."

"*What?* Then find him. Tell him to meet me at the diner for lunch. And Chick?"

"Yes?"

"I'm taking the rest of the day off. When I come in tomorrow I want that wall finished and all the crap out of the office."

"But—"

"Finished, you hear me?"

"Yes sir. I mean, yes."

Lynn had already ordered his burger by the time I reached the diner. I got right to the point: I wanted decent space and I wanted it now. Chick could stay, but from here on out I had final say in all my staffing decisions.

Lynn was amused. "A man who takes the bull by the balls. That's good," he said. "Hiring, fine. Chick's a nice guy—"

"That's not the point."

"—but the space thing's a little tricky. It may not be apparent to you, Jon, but we're in a bit of an economic slump at the moment. Since the Soviets went bust, the President's got a false sense of security, you know what I mean, and he's scaling back the defense budget. Now don't get me wrong, *your* project's a priority here—"

"Then give me what I need to do the job."

Lynn laughed. "Easier said than done, boyo."

I pulled a plane ticket from my coat pocket and slapped it on the table. "Then I'm gone," I said. "I don't have the time or the patience to fuck around."

After the shock gave way, anger and respect for me fought for control of his face. "All right," he said finally. He smiled. "I'll see what I can do."

Immediately I began mapping other strategies. The plane ticket wouldn't work twice.

When I discovered a video store in town I had second thoughts about a film series. Would people pay to see old movies when they could rent them and take them home? The store's selection was poor—westerns, splatter films, dumb sex comedies—but its business was brisk.

One night I rented *Pat Garrett and Billy the Kid.* The real Pat Garrett once lived on what's now the White Sands Missile Range in southern New Mexico; a bomb site occupies the spot where Billy made a daring jailbreak.

In Peckinpah's movie, James Coburn as Pat Garrett rides into town knowing he's probably going to kill his old pal Billy. They'd been outlaws together, but Garrett's turned a corner. He's the sheriff now. Billy (Kris Kristofferson) knocks back a drink, then sneers at his friend. "So, Pat, what's it feel like to be on the side of the law?" he asks.

Coburn looks at him.

As the video rolled across my TV screen that night, shock-waves rocked my trailer. My children stirred.

"It feels like times have changed."

Of course, I didn't bring art to Tilton. The place had its own very American sense of style: *Penthouse* desk calendars instead of *The Naked Maja*, celebrity photos taped to cash registers or white pine walls instead of statues in the center of town.

That first day I'd noticed Jack Dempsey's picture in the diner, framed above the counter along with the glossies of missiles. He was on the menu, too. The "Dempsey Delight," a BLT with a dollop of horseradish.

The Tilton Hotel had a sign in its lobby that said Dempsey

had lived there one spring, back in 1914. The building didn't look that old.

It turns out, Dempsey was all over Nevada, in sketches, photos, historical markers. Over half the towns in the state claim to be his birthplace. Eventually I read he was born in Colorado, but he made a name for himself throughout the West, boxing in coal towns, mining camps, railroad stops, taking all comers, proving himself King of the Rockies long before he became heavyweight champion of the world. For $2.50 one night, in front of a tubercular audience of miners (and one or two lapsed Mormons) in the back room of a Tonapah saloon, he battled Big Johnny Sudenberg to a draw. Though he was knocked down repeatedly that night, he knew from then on that no one could stop him. By bathing his fists in beef brine and chewing pine resin to toughen his jaw, Dempsey became as hard as the West.

Clearly, he was still the god of this place. A hunched, iconic figure with a cowboy's face and a laborer's build; a vision of propulsion, ready to fire his left and right. With narrow eyes and a full-lipped frown he dared the world to come get him. A brash American youngster. A god of conflict.

He was a favorite of Lynn's. The day we were supposed to move into our house, Lynn stopped by the trailer to help us carry our bags. Our furniture was in storage. He said, "You folks're sure lucky. This new home is top-of-the-line, comfort-wise. White wooden trim, central air, brick patio out back—"

"I'll bet Dempsey lived there," I said.

"What's that?"

"He lived everywhere else, didn't he?"

Lynn stiffened. "Listen, Jon, you can kid all you want, but the man was a bona fide hero. He went from being a bum to being champ to becoming a Hollywood actor."

"Top-of-the-line, American Dream–wise," Peg said.

Our house was indeed lovely. Sliding glass doors opened

onto a beautiful, artificially forested hillside. Someone had already hung a wind chime over the built-in barbecue grill. Stained-glass windows (irises, lilies) shaded the brown and white kitchen tiles.

We hung our clothes in the closets, plugged in the television. Dana left Bernie sitting on a pillow in the living room.

Lynn followed us back to the trailer for a second load. When we returned to the house a half hour later, the driveway was blocked by two black trucks. Three men in airtight suits and helmets marched single-file out of the front hall, closing the door behind them. Yellow slime smeared their boots. Dana grabbed my hand.

Lynn had a whispered conversation with General Thompson, the man who'd interviewed me months ago. He was standing by one of the trucks. A few minutes later, Lynn told me to return to the trailer.

"What's happened?" I said.

He cleared his throat officiously. "Seems there's been a rupture underground. A substance yet to be identified has begun to leak through some of the floorboards."

I'd picked up his jargon. "A *hot* substance?"

"At this point we can neither confirm nor deny—"

"My family could've—"

"Jon, let's just get back to the trailer, all right?"

I'd been holding a small bag. I tossed it across the lawn. "You said you knew the lay of the land."

"It's inexplicable," Lynn said.

Dana tugged at my sleeve. "Daddy, Bernie's in there." She pointed at the house.

"No ma'am," Lynn told her, anticipating her question. "We can't go back inside now."

"Daddy, it's Bernie."

"Honey, the house isn't safe." I glared at General Thompson, who pretended not to notice me.

Dana stared at the men in suits, who seemed to belong on the moon. "They're going to hurt Bernie!"

I leaned close to Lynn. "Dempsey," I whispered.

"What?"

"Don't drop your guard, Major. When you least expect it, I'm going to punch your fucking lights out."

SOMETIMES at night now I hear the women chant. I'll be sitting in a lawn chair in front of the trailer, trying to find static-free reception on my radio. Even the Vegas stations with all their juice get lost in scratchy bursts, layered whispers, musical blats that float in and out as if spinning in a dust devil's gut. Occasionally a single station will lock in for five minutes before it's over-whelmed by other voices or the hot, empty howling in the air around Tilton. Oldies slide into funk into rap. Heavy-metal murk gives way to the whine of a pedal steel.

Lately, between songs, in those rare moments of clarity, I've heard a series of ads sponsored by the DOE.

"Nuclear waste: could a traffic accident cause it to leak?" a woman asks in one of the frequently repeated spots. "I'm Ron Nayman," a man replies softly. "And the answer is no. Nuclear waste is transported in pellet form. So you see, there's nothing to leak!" A chirping melody, like the theme from the old *Donna Reed Show*, rises—then I lose it all to static.

Ron Nayman is a popular Las Vegas sportscaster. His easy manner could make Armageddon sound like halftime entertain-ment. His sound bites for the DOE are prepared (for a tasty sum, I've read) by a Nevada PR firm that also serves *anti*nuclear groups.

The Vegas mentality: cover all bets.

Most nights at sunset, women begin to gather at the edge of

the Test Site: Hopi women, Navajo women all the way from Tucson, Yuma, Tuba City, Carlsbad, Window Rock; college girls up from UNLV, feminists, Peace Movement workers—they come to grieve the nuclear presence. From time to time a man'll show, but the vigils are primarily woman-centered. "We're the conscience of the race," Peg says. "Men are its burden."

She's kidding me, but not entirely. I don't entirely disagree.

All night, small bands of women will huddle on hills overlooking Jackass Flats. There, on two mesas called Skull and Little Skull, barrels of submarine-reactor sediment, shipped regularly from California, lie exposed to desert breezes. Other groups will get as close as they safely can to the sump ponds near Yucca Mountain, where displaced earth and water are stored to make room for underground drilling. Still others will station themselves on mesas near Frenchman Lake, from which they can see the skeletons of "doom town" houses, bridges, and towers, melted and collapsed from the forces of nuclear winds.

Withery Joshua trees pepper the flats; dust-encrusted army tanks, saturated after nearly forty years with still-active alpha particles, sink into salt-white sand.

The women light candles, sway together and chant:

> Listen.
> We know that when you come, we'll die.
> Listen.
> We know that when you come, we'll die.

As a blessing for the land they sing Navajo songs of the earth:

> May it be beautiful, my house the earth;
> From my head, may it be beautiful;
> To my feet, may it be beautiful;
> All above me, may it be beautiful;
> All around me, may it be so.

When I switch off my radio I hear them if the breezes are right: lovely voices sailing through panes of quarter-moonlight. Sometimes Peg drives over to join them. I'll tuck the kids into bed. Scott's been calm, but he sleeps too much. Dana still mourns Bernie. Peg bought her a new stuffed toy, but our baby girl won't touch it. "Dad, what does radiation look like?" she asked me the other night.

"You can't see it," I said.

"Oh. Sort of like whatever's in Scott's brain that makes him crazy."

"Your brother's not crazy."

"*He* says he is."

I straightened the sheet at her feet. "No. He just has to work hard each day to be happy."

"Are you happy, Daddy?"

"Yes, sweetie. As long as you and Scott and your mother are here, I am. Now go to sleep."

On the nights when Peg's at the Test Site I hammer an old punching bag I bought one day at the "New and Used" store downtown. It's a toy, really, mildewy, lumpy in places, hung on a chain in the middle of a large freestanding tripod. I've set the whole thing up out back, by the trailer's water heater. Right crosses, left uppercuts. A rigid scowl like Dempsey's.

I work up a sweat and feel good about myself. Then I blow the whole regimen by lighting a cigarette. I'm cutting back on them, though.

Peg says I should join her at the Test Site. Once I did, and enjoyed communing with all those strong, sorrowful women who've pledged themselves to cleaning the earth. But later I felt sad. For all their beauty, their candles and songs don't achieve any more than I do, slamming the bag. The ladies cheer *themselves* up. They can say they've done something.

But the blasts still come.

Tonight the water heater hisses like a man out of breath, about to go down in the ring. Its pilot light casts a pale blue pool at my feet. I'm wincing at pains in my ribs, struggling with a cheap canvas bag, a smoker's body, and a set of manly values that, magnified, has led to all this poison in the desert.

I'm forty-four years old, I think. I'm hurting, and with my weak, throbbing fists I'll kill anyone who threatens my family.

Peg says I'm wrong: vigils and nonviolent rituals *do* effect change. "Women understand this better than men, I think. Making something with silence and patience—like a quilt," she says. "Or a child."

"Right. Men are ogres—"

"Stop kidding. I just meant there's enormous power in stillness."

One example, she says. Last month, fifty Shoshone-Bannock women from southern Idaho intercepted a truck hauling spent nuclear fuel from a Colorado weapons plant. They sat in the road and refused to allow it to cross their reservation; the waste returned to its source. *That* vigil paid off.

But distances are so vast in the West—who's to say what's happening, and where, at any given hour? How do we know what to raise our voices against?

Lynn told me the Site tested bombs every twelve days, but it's more like eight. The singing women have noticed bright pulses in the sky. Gushing walls of heat. I've experienced these too. Still, none of the country's major dailies have run accounts of resumed atmospheric testing.

Lynn will neither confirm nor deny, etc.

Does anyone outside of Nye County know what's going on here? To the rest of the nation we're a dust bowl, a small population far from the business hub of the East, with little muscle in D.C.

Why should anyone care what happens to Nevada?

My knuckles stiffen. Pain spreads in my chest, and I grab myself through my shirt. I'm pushing too hard tonight. I reach to stop the swinging bag. My body's like a chart, each ache a mark indicating old character flaws that have hardened like bone spurs, old strengths that have withered away.

As I cool down and deny myself a Marlboro Light, for years my mother's brand, I remember her sunken mouth and cheeks, her flittering thoughts, and again I mourn her diminishment. I slam the punching bag a couple more times. How do you know when your own mind starts to go? I think. Tanked up on the bad air here, maybe I've already started to slip; maybe the symptoms won't show for several months. Then what? Will I bump into the oil field woman? Invent phantom lovers for Peg?

On the breezes from the Test Site I hear the women's voices. One of my knuckles is bleeding. I grab a pair of Jumbo Baggies from the kitchen, fill them with ice, and wrap them around my hands. I sit in the lawn chair with the radio off.

A falling star.

I remember my father telling me as a boy not to worry, they can't hurt you. Most meteors, he said, are the size of safety pins.

After midnight the desert turns cold. Ice water leaks from the Baggies onto my sneakers and knees. Crickets make music in the sage.

I watch a plane drift low for its airport approach. Its blinking wing lights are like little benedictions in the dark.

Much later, Peg pulls up in the car.

"I heard you singing," I tell her.

She doesn't want to talk. She's heard sounds on the plains of the Site, metallic clanging in the shadows. "Hold me," she says. She says something's about to happen.

We sit together in the sand. In the next instant the sky's on fire, but only for a moment. Another routine explosion.

Then another.

In the trailer Dana starts to cry. We go in to her together. She reaches for Peg, who rocks her. "What will our survivors, if there are any, say of us?" Peg asks me, or herself. She lifts our daughter out of bed. A third blast sears the Dipper. "Will they say we were crazy or just plain hateful of each other?"

When Dana's finally asleep and Peg's in bed I walk outside again, light the night's last cigarette. What will they say of us? That we were brilliant, I think. Unflappable and luminous.

They'll say we were gods.

They'll say we were born wrong.

6

"KNOCK-KNOCK." Lynn walked into my office early one morning. "Anybody here?" he said.

"In back," I called. The workmen had finished the wall, replaced my desk with a new mahogany monster, and at my request added a private alcove so I could shut myself away, work in peace, make uninterrupted telephone calls. I'd hired a secretary, a woman named Tommie. When Lynn arrived that morning, she and Chick were next door, supervising changes in the gym. Lynn hadn't delivered the extra space I'd wanted—the basketball court would have to be our theater.

He offered his hand and I shook it. "Coffee?"

"Love some," he said. "Thought I'd drop by, see how you're doing."

I swept my arm around the outer room: piled carpet, scattered file drawers, two dead ivy plants (Chick was supposed to water them but didn't). "As you see," I said.

Lynn emptied a packet of Sweet'n Low into his cup. "Actually, I know you're feeling a bit disgruntled, Jon. I thought you might want to talk. Don't blame you, of course. It's hard enough to adjust to a new job, new place, new schools for the kids . . . then that house mess happens. I'm awfully sorry about that. Did you get reimbursed for the clothes you lost? And what else was it? A television, I believe?"

"My little girl's stuffed bear," I said. "She'll never forgive me."

"I'm really very sorry. We're scouting out another location for you. The new house'll be just as nice as the first one was. I guarantee it." He blew on his coffee. His skin was wrinkle-free; this made him look smooth but not exactly young. "I don't suppose you've had time yet to plan any special arts galas for us?"

"I don't have enough cash." I said this as sharply as I could without sounding rude. "But as a matter of fact . . ." I led him back to the alcove where I'd tacked to the wall a series of sketches showing our planned theater; next to those I'd hung rough storyboards for possible productions of Our Town and Waiting for Godot. I had a director friend in Texas who'd recently staged a Beckett festival in Austin. As a favor to me, he said, he'd come out and work for less than scale. Godot required minimal costuming and props—torn coats, an old tree. Besides, the play's barren (postnuclear?) setting and its bleak humor—

ESTRAGON: Nothing to be done.
VLADIMIR: I'm beginning to come 'round to that opinion.

—seemed right on the money for Tilton. I wasn't naive, though: Beckett off the bat would be too much for this place. It was a mistake to underestimate people just because they lived in small communities. In fact, I'd had great success, in the past, introducing avant-garde art to places like Ardmore, Oklahoma, and Lufkin, Texas. Still, it was best to warm up with something a little less imaginative. Earn the town's trust.

Lynn sat. "So if we got you a bigger budget, got you settled into a nice place, things'd be okay? Or better, at least? We could be friends?" He smiled.

I worried that befriending him would be a little like befriending nuclear waste. Dangerous if I got too close. And what was in it for him? Surely more than the fact that he'd seen Patton and thought I could turn him into George C. Scott. I got the feeling he'd crawled out on a limb in supporting the arts, and he'd lose face with the brass if I didn't work out.

I poured myself more coffee. "Can I be frank with you, Major?"

A jackhammer shook the floor next door. He said, "Lynn, Jon. *At ease* here, buddy, all right? Talk to me."

"All right, Lynn. I'm concerned about my family."

"How's that?"

"The army's resumed atmospheric testing here at the Site, hasn't it?"

"I told you—"

"I know. The Limited Test Ban Treaty. I also know what my eyes and ears tell me. I don't understand how you've kept it out of the news, or why people in town aren't talking about it."

"You're not in any danger, if that's what's bothering you," Lynn said.

"So you *are*—"

"I didn't say that." He took off his cap.

"We weren't in any danger in our house, either," I said. "You assured me. Next thing we know, a prehistoric swamp swallows everything we own."

"Jon—"

"Don't patronize me, okay?" I was up and pacing the room. I knew I was about to be reckless but I didn't care: weeks of frustration—and fear of the blasts—had finally burst. For days now I'd barely managed not to snap at Peg and the kids, the most convenient targets in my heated moments. "I didn't come here to eat your goddam poison," I said.

He stood. "That's enough. I've been very patient with you, Jon—"

"Is that so? Your people treat me like I'm a dumb grunt, Major. Well, screw that. And I'll tell you something else: you wouldn't know a work of art if it bit you in the ass." I was kissing my job goodbye—I knew it—but the invective wouldn't stop. "I don't know why we're even talking, you and me. In the arts we share ideas, but you wouldn't understand that, would you? When *you* boys get your paws around a thought, you seal it, cover it up, classify it so no one'll know it's there—"

He aimed a finger at my head. "That's right, friend, and what you don't know fills volumes. So keep your fucking mouth shut."

"We're talking lives here, the human heart—"

"The human heart? The human *heart*? You know how many ways there are to get at the human heart? Man, the piece I'm carrying could *waste* your goddam—" He stopped himself. His face was red and as bright as a late Matisse. He composed his features and smiled. I caught my breath. "Well," he said, smoothing his cap. He tried a different approach. "Okay. Let's just calm down here, all right? I understand your fear, Jon. Really, I do."

A huge silence, like a ship's sail, hung inside me.

Lynn spoke softly now. "Listen to me—I'm not an insensitive man. I've devoted my whole life to the army, and sometimes I forget that we in the military take certain things for granted—like the need for nuclear testing—that others may disagree with." He walked over and examined my sketches of the theater. I didn't trust him, especially after his outburst; I watched his hands.

"I also understand that a man like yourself, a man married to the arts, with a love of beauty, may see the military as a hellish machine, menacing nature and culture. It's not surprising to me that so many artists lean to the political left. But you see, that's why we brought you here. The town needs balance. We're not haters of beauty, Jon. But sometimes we do forget to stop and appreciate what I hope you can offer us. And if you'll let me, maybe I can give *you* a sense of balance too."

The room was hot. My shirt stuck to my skin. "How? What do you mean?"

He shrugged. "If you're game, I'd like to show you around the state, take you over into Colorado and Wyoming, tour you through some of the DOE's facilities. I'm sure we can clear it through General Thompson. Tilton may not look like much to a newcomer, but it's a vital link in a long chain of communities devoted to our national security. We're proud of the role we play. Eventually, I'd like to see some of that pride rub off on you."

The man was completely sincere. "If you think you can turn me into a warrior, Major, forget it," I said.

"No. I just want to show you around. Increase your understanding, that's all."

"I need to pull these productions together."

"Of course. We can go anytime you like." He pulled two yellow tickets out of his coat pocket. "In the meantime, I'd be delighted if you'd accompany me to the football game this Friday night. We're very excited about our Tilton High Cougars," he said. "The smart boys in Vegas say they've got a legitimate shot at the state championship this year. We could meet at the stadium, say, seven-thirty. Grab some Cokes and dogs, talk some more about your ideal budget, okay?"

I felt weary all the sudden. His kindness was just another tactic. In my head I heard my father's voice telling me again it's good to be scared. Fear increases all your senses. Keeps you alert. But with a seasoned fighter like Lynn, I didn't know what to look for. How would he strike? Like a missile in the night, I thought. My stomach clenched. What was it, really, I feared? This man bore me no ill will. Yet he and his team were steadily spoiling the desert—an act that hit me as a personal violation.

To the army the land was merely property, an abstract grid . . . certainly nothing as romantic as the wild frontier. Lynn's desire to indoctrinate me didn't bother me as much as the coldness with which I imagined a soldier sees all things.

"You *like* football?" he asked.

I had to understand his motives. "Sure," I said. "I'd love to see a game."

"Great. Isn't your boy in the high school?" he asked.

"Yes."

"How's he doing?"

"No problems." Fingers crossed.

"Good, good. You know, I've seen that movie, *Our Town.* Bill Holden."

"Right."

"The fellow who walks around introducing everyone . . . it's a small part, but real important. Is it the same in the play?"

"The Stage Manager, yes."

He grinned shyly. "Well. All right, then. I'll see you Friday. Hi to your wife."

I didn't see Peg until after sunset. I knew she'd be anxious—we were having dinner that evening with Zack and Beth Heron, a couple we'd met and liked in town. At five, when I tried to leave the office, Chick called me into the gym, where the builders were putting the final touches on the stage. Rough warps bubbled the wood. "Impossible," I told him. "Actors can't perform on this. They'll fall and break their necks. And look at these seats!"

That week I'd gambled and bought, unseen, three hundred chairs from a closed-down casino. On the phone, the salesman had promised me they were fine, but their backs were locked in a forward position. They looked like tongue depressors jammed into the ground. Welcome to the State of Chance, where money disappears like stupid hopes. I'd trusted the casino man the way tourists gassing up in Tilton, headed for Vegas, trusted luck. They tasted margaritas in the salty breeze, heard lusty bedsprings in the overheated wheezing of their engines.

Clearly, I wasn't going to make it home right away; I had to huddle with the workers, sketch alternatives, readjust the budget. *Our Town* seemed remote.

I called Peg. No answer.

Tommie, the new secretary, assumed my instructions meant *yards,* not *feet,* between the audience and the orchestra pit.

"Why would you assume that?" I asked. My anger at Lynn burned my face still.

Tommie was a small woman in her late forties. Pleasant phone voice, solid word-processing experience. Keep her away from numbers, I thought. She stammered, "I just—I sort of—"

"Do me a favor, Tommie. Don't make assumptions. Come to me first, okay?"

For twenty minutes, then, I had to assure her I wasn't letting her go. I spoke a foreign language here. My ambitions, my aesthetic inclinations, my needs were completely at odds with this community. I understood how artists felt exiled from the very cultures they lived in.

It was nearly seven when I finally got away. The Herons expected us at eight. I sped down Main Street, past the park my family had seen the night we first arrived in town. The grizzled man in the raincoat and sweater was there. He'd built a fire with sagebrush and paper. I was used to homeless men in cities, but this fellow was an anomaly in Tilton. Most folks here were on the government dole; poverty wasn't a local issue.

The park man watched me pass. He held his hands to the flames.

Peg had been shopping when I called. I apologized for the delay, squeezed by the kids, reaching for my closet. The trailer was cluttered with schoolbooks, shoes, stockings, boxes. Our new television buzzed in the corner: the President singing hymns to capital punishment.

"House the homeless," I grumbled at the set, testy in my haste. "That'll drop your damn crime rate. Peg, where's my gray jacket?"

She studied my face. "Okay, kids, out of the trailer," she said. "Your father and I have to get dressed. Out, out. A little privacy, please."

Scott and Dana went groaning into the dusk.

"Not too far!" I called after them. "I'll be ready in a jiffy if—"

"Slow down, Jon."

"But—"

She put her hands on my shoulders. "You need to relax," she said. "I can help."

"Oh you can, can you? You think—?"

"Yes, if we hurry." She kissed me lightly. "I hate to see you come home like this every day."

"I'm working with the reality-impaired," I said.

"Show me the magic in those fingers."

She was out of her clothes in a snap. I knew this wasn't just for me. We both needed more intimacy than we'd been able to steal lately. Plus, she needed assurance. These days she thought of herself as an "aging dancer," and made bitter jokes about her "craters and sags." After eighteen years of marriage, I loved her richly historied skin.

She stepped backward onto the couch, slipped her fingers between her legs. "What do you see?" she said.

I smiled. "Nothing. My mind and eyes are chaste."

Breasts dipping this way and that. Moist skin. Parted lips. With a fluid twist, like the lovesick mermaid in *Ondine*, her favorite ballet, she straddled me and rubbed my thighs with her wrists. "I love you," I said. "I love you I love you I love you."

Sweating, we rolled in a pile of pillows onto the floor. Her short black hair brushed my cheeks; her breasts, like sweetly scented packets of potpourri, slid up and down my chest.

One of our stomachs gurgled, I couldn't tell whose, then we came together all at once. Our arms and legs fell helplessly back against the cushions. Breathless, she pledged her life to me.

Crickets were beginning to *chrrr* when we pulled into town. Televised sports cheers drifted through open windows. Soap and kitchen smells. Somewhere, a lawn mower gritted its teeth.

The Herons lived in a flat wooden duplex not far from the hill Lynn had pointed out to me that first day in the diner. The houses here still had Christmas lights in their eaves, though Christmas had been over for months. Zack worked as a process operator at Mesa Bend, a plant that specialized in plutonium bomb triggers. He'd been a janitor until recently, when the plant offered him a raise—ten cents an hour—to assist researchers in the "hot" labs. He figured the risk was worth it; the plant was fastidious about safety. "We respect the materials we work with," he told me. "That's all you've got to do." He was a big man about my age, maybe a little older, trim but beginning to lose his battle to stay in shape. His waistline and upper chest were relaxing. Fit but on the edge.

His wife, Beth, worked in a day-care center. She was tiny and tense, like a chicken. Her mother, Midge, shared the duplex. Midge had lived in Tilton all her life—before it was called Tilton, before there was even a town. Her father had been a lifer in the army. As a young woman in the fifties she'd witnessed the first atmospheric tests at the Site.

Zack poured wine—then 7-Up for Scott and Dana. They looked edgy and bored. Midge passed me a tray of Velveeta and saltine crackers.

"So," Zack said, dropping into a green recliner. "Are you settling in?"

"It's been a hard adjustment for us," I admitted.

"I'll bet, with all that racket out at the Site. Where you're living you must hear it all the time."

I nodded. "The army swears it's all underground, but—"

"No, I'm talking about that silly chanting. The singing business, with all those crazy women."

Peg blushed. She told him she admired those women and joined them whenever she could.

Zack sputtered into his wineglass. He tried to apologize. He didn't mean anything personal, he said, he just didn't see the point of it all.

"It's like a funeral service," Peg said—almost a whisper. "The ritual helps heal us."

Zack pressed her. "Surely you don't expect to stop the testing?" he said.

"Who knows?" Peg smiled sadly. "The music provides a structure for focusing our passion—it's like beaming sunlight through a lens. Concentrating the effort."

"Well now, I can't say much about singing," Zack said. "But I *do* think the testing's necessary. So I guess we disagree, Peg. I feel safer knowing my country's out to protect us."

Beth emerged from the kitchen with some fried, puffy things heaving and spitting on a tray. "An experiment," she said. "Hope you like 'em."

We didn't have much in common with the Herons, but I found myself relaxing with them, enjoying their company. I asked Midge if these recent blasts reminded her of the old days.

"Oh hell yes. The army's out there punching holes in the stratosphere again." She said this with the tired, defiant air of a woman who's seen everything in life and doesn't give a damn about any of it anymore. "I used to wonder why the sun rose twice a day. But back then, you know, when they first started, it was more exciting than scary to us. We didn't know anything about gamma rays, or whatever the hell they're called."

Scott squirmed on the couch. He crunched the ice in his glass with volume and precision.

Midge said that she and her husband, may he rest in peace, owned the first profitable ranch in Tilton, in the early sixties. "We used to find payloads in our barn manure," she said. "You never knew what'd drop out of the sky." She told us that one morning she was in a corral with her favorite white mare when a silver F-15 careened like a wounded eagle overhead and fired a Sidewinder missile at an invisible target in the distance. "Son-of-a-bitch pilots used the peak of our barn as a landmark to turn for home," Midge said. "This boy was so close that day I could see right into the cockpit, right into his little green eyes." The jet spooked the mare, who kicked Midge through a fence. She lifted her blouse for us. Permanent red scars marred her flesh, just below her heart.

"Gross," Dana whispered. Scott spit ice into his glass.

Beth called us all to the dinner table. Cauliflower with cheddar cheese, collard greens, fried okra, mashed potatoes. Cherry cobbler for dessert.

Peg didn't eat much. She seemed as distracted as the kids. After a tense silence she asked Zack what his work was like. He said eight hours a day he dissolved plutonium in acid, transformed it into a solid, separated the solid into pieces he called "hockey pucks," then fired them in a furnace purged with argon gas. "The fact that it's potentially dangerous makes it kind of fun," he said.

I asked him what he'd always wanted to be as a child. "Did you ever imagine you'd do what you're doing now?"

He wiped his lips. "I didn't even know this stuff was here," he said. "I *still* don't know how it works."

Midge said, "My boys wanted to be rodeo cowboys. But the money's all dried up. You *got* to join the government here. They're the only ones with cash now."

Throughout the meal I'd been aware of Scott's heavy breathing. Now he looked ill. I reached for his arm. "Are you all right, son?"

Without warning he shook off my hand, stood, and pushed back his chair. His neck turned bright red. He wagged a finger at Midge. "And what does the government *do* with all its cash, huh?" He was shouting. Dana hid her face. "Wipe out crime? House the homeless? No! Not a fucking chance! So there you go." He rushed past me, jostling the table, kicked open the kitchen door, and headed for the hills.

Peg and I both jumped up. "I've got him," I said. She sat back down and wrapped her arms around Dana.

Scott had already run past the last residential street east of town before I glimpsed him. He was slipping on a rocky slope, trying to climb a hill.

I fell several times trying to balance myself on the incline. Scott's fingers were bleeding; tears mixed with dirty sweat on his face. I finally reached him halfway up, snagged a belt loop on his jeans, and pulled him down to me, into a hug. He was sobbing and screaming all at once. "Shhh, shhh," I whispered. A dust cloud settled around us.

Of course I'd recognized my own words in his outburst: my stupid remark tonight when I'd yelled at the television. It was unnerving to hear my comments—my most deeply held beliefs—twisted into disease.

It was unbearable to watch my son crumble.

"Scott, Scottie, it's all right, honey. Take it easy here," I said into his shirt.

"I'm sorry, Dad, but—it's just—everything's shit, everything's shit, Dad, and I can't—"

"I'm with you, son. I'm right here. We'll tackle it together, all right? Whatever it is. Whatever happens. Just take it easy. It's okay now."

A hawk circled above us. Children's laughter rose from the streets below.

I told him to remember the mourning doves' peaceful calls in the woods near our old Oregon house, the ocean's rainbow swells.

Eventually his body stopped jerking and I thought he'd cried himself to sleep. I sat there not moving, gripping him tightly. I took a breath and watched the sky stay absolutely still.

Dana and Peg and the Herons had gathered in a small circle in a field directly below us. After about ten minutes I shook Scott gently, asked if he was okay to go back home. He nodded. I took his hand and we half walked, half slid down the hill.

SCOTT always loved the mourning doves cooing in the valley below our farmhouse in Oregon. In the spring, hummingbirds erupted out of evening light, then quickly disappeared near the sugar-water feeder on our deck. Scott stood, clapping his hands on the sliding glass door, shrieking with delight at the flashing feathers and at his own smudged fingerprints on the pane.

I remember the smell of garlic bread; Peg baking in the kitchen. I'd ladle warm soup into bowls as smooth and curved as the small of her back.

Down the street, neighbor children giggled, playing hide-and-seek in salmon-colored fog. It rolled slow as a thresher over houselight-dotted hills. The children crouched behind sugar pines and thimbleberry. Their parents' voices rose from bright kitchens. "Boys! Dinner's ready! Tell your sisters!"

I told my son, "Hey partner, let's eat."

Each night, feeling grateful, feeling lucky to be where I was, I'd take silent stock of the house. Cut flowers blooming in a swan-necked vase. Lemons stacked in a copper bowl. On a paper lamp-shade in the living room, a brown spot like a bruise where it had touched the low-watt bulb.

My wife's soft breathing in bed; my son slapping water in his soapy evening bath.

These are my keepsakes, I'd think.

These are what I've made of my life.

I'd run a rubber duck up one of Scottie's arms, then down his bubbly other. He'd grab the toy from my hands, squeeze its head until it sang. A long, slow hiss of air.

Now, as I sift through these memories I wonder, What did I miss? Wouldn't a better father have seen the seeds of his son's awful pain?

But where was it, that darkness, those glorious days on the coast? I recall only happiness. One morning Scott noticed a clump of black-eyed Susans in the V of a wizened cypress trunk—as if the gray, salt-eaten tree were offering a bouquet of wild thanks to the world before it crumbled and departed. Osprey, terns, and cormorants practiced figure eights in the air. When they rested on sunny rocks above the waves the cormorants looked like bowling pins. Anemones, purple and gray in foamy tidal pools full of sea-polished pebbles, parted their sexual lips. Ocean worms, plankton, horseneck clams, cockles, and crabs, abundant, luxurious kelp . . . all moist with the sweet, warm smell of new life, wriggling, and decay. . . .

Scottie laughed and laughed in the sun. Below us, on niches in the cliff, sea lions sunbathed and brayed. Bleached-to-bone-white driftwood splintered in spray.

Peg and I used to tell each other, "This is Eden."

Then *this* must be the Fall.

Once, after an especially loud and violent episode, I asked Scott to describe his pain. "It's a pressure in my head," he said. "Fire in my eyes. I don't always know when it's coming or what'll set it off. I just know the world seems out of control, Dad. It seems so inadequate."

There's a scene in Arthur Penn's famous western *The Left-Handed Gun* in which Paul Newman as Billy the Kid mourns his boss on the cattle trail. (Newman overplays the role, with a touch of James Dean angst.) A rival cowpunching gang in cahoots with an evil sheriff shoots Mr. Tunstull in the back. Billy finds his body, drops to the ground, and falls into tears. He hears the assassins' horses running in the distance. He stands. He looks at the swelling sky as if the West's too big to comprehend, its runneled flat prairies, its lawlessness, its funneling heat. He slaps his left thigh where his pistol's usually strapped. He isn't wearing it now, but again and again he strokes the leg. Then the camera pans back and he's swallowed in the dusty white landscape.

That's how I felt, cradling my son in the desert.

That night, on our way home from the Herons', Scott slept in the backseat. He'd exhausted himself on the hill. Dana hummed an Aerosmith tune. Peg and I watched the black road absorb our headlights. I'd taken a different route from before, trying to find a shortcut back to our trailer.

In a sheep field I'd never seen I glimpsed a sign. "Abel Oil Corporation," it said, and below that, "The Jack Dempsey. Restricted. Keep Out." Two sheared lambs nibbled grass at its base.

Less than a mile beyond the sign I felt an irregular rumble, from a copper draw west of the road. The highway shook. I slowed the car. Peg asked, "What is it?"

"I don't know," I said. "It feels like—"

She screamed. A curved metallic wall rose in front of us, out of the ground. Blinking lights. A zigzag motion. I lost control of the wheel and skidded us onto the road's gravel shoulder. Dust poured through my open window. Except for throbbing lights I couldn't tell what was out there. My heart hurt in its pounding.

"Mom, what's *that?*" Dana said, excited and frightened. She crawled over the backseat.

Peg shook. "I'm not sure, honey. Stay down."

"A UFO? Are we going to Mars? Mom!"

The noise was above us now. The car seemed frail as paper, an origami animal about to be twisted apart. Like the first missile test outside our trailer, the roar rattled my skull. I searched for Peg's hand.

Scott stirred but didn't wake. The lights circled behind us. I noticed wings, a steady hum. Then as quickly as the thing had appeared it was gone.

No one was talking—not our friends, not my colleagues at work, not the army. The implication was we hadn't seen *anything* on the road.

"Moonlight mirage," Lynn told me over breakfast in the diner. "That silver light on the rocks—sometimes you think you see movement. The highway looks like metal." He buttered his toast.

It was easy to laugh at Lynn's manner, but he wasn't always the caricature I'm afraid I've made him in these pages, to convey the effect of his presence. Some days he was just another guy doing his job, hoping to marry, raise a family. At other times, he became a jargon storm like the man I've presented here—I never knew what would set him off. Clearly, my glimpse of the plane, or whatever it was, upset him. He stammered and launched into an outlandish story to distract me.

"You want *real* believe-it-or-nots, you should've seen my Grandpa Percy's ranch up in Montana," he said. "Perce was a retired air force colonel, a second father to me, but his place was damn scary. He told me a story once, said it was back in 1908 or '10, I think it was. Halley's comet was blazing away in the sky and my Grandma May had just had her baby prematurely. In the first five minutes it aged six years. When it was ten minutes old it began to sprout whiskers. Standing at the foot of the bed, Perce said, he thought he was going to vomit. Its body never grew but its skin loosened, hair turned gray, teeth yellowed and fell out. 'It's the comet,' said the midwife. 'Evil moon's cursed this miserable child.' No one knew if it was a boy or a girl."

He shook his head. "Finally May sat up in her four-poster—an amazing strong woman—and hurled the thing out the window into a putrid black ditch. In the next few minutes the baby shriveled up and died in a trickle of water and cow fur and leaves." He laughed. "So you never know what you'll find—or imagine—out here. Desert's a spooky old place. Got to take it all in stride. We still on for Friday night?"

"Lynn," I said, "I know the difference between fairy tales and fighter planes."

He waved a stick of bacon in my face. "My friend, you got a bad attitude problem, you know that? I'll say it again. I'm here to help you. I believe you owe me a little more respect than you've shown to this point." He sliced the rind off a small cantaloupe. "I mean, it's not all treasure, okay, nothing ever is. Let me paint you a picture, Jon. Say there's a guy, a normal guy someplace—I don't know—*average*, okay? All day he wrestles with bond issues, buyouts, leverages, tax wrinkles, crap like that. Is this the fatted calf for him? This guy, he's maybe forty-five, fifty, all right? Is this his city of Oz? No. But hell, he studies that wrinkle anyway, because who knows, you know? And he leaves everything else alone because it's not for him. Maybe Oz is off-limits for a *reason*, see, this fellow, he—"

"What are you talking about?" I said.

He snapped up the check. "I'm talking about flexibility, Jon. The intelligence to know when to quit your line of pursuit. That's what my Grandpa Perce always said. Can't win a battle without it." He gave me a tight smile. "Same holds true for civilians."

Meanwhile, Scott had missed three days of class. He'd been mopey and quiet all week, not sleeping.

"So tell me," I said one night.

He looked at me. "Tell you what?"

"Whatever it is."

He shrugged.

"Would you like to see another doctor?"

"Right. So they can fuck me up on drugs all over again."

"We wouldn't let that happen. No more drugs."

He picked at his sleeve. "Dad, this is the *only* job you could find?"

"Right now, yes. What's the matter? You don't like this place?"

"Do you?"

"Not much, no."

"Then why do we stay?" he said.

"You know why. Money's tight. And there's nothing else out there for me. I've been trying."

"You should've been a lawyer or something."

"I should've been King of the World, but I'm not."

"We're probably being poisoned right now. That thing you saw the other night—"

"Scott, there's a whole lot of stuff I can't control," I said. "I'm sorry life's not any easier. We'll just have to pull together."

"What if that's not good enough?"

"You tell me."

Peg insisted I was too hard on him. We both feared he might try to hurt himself again. Last time it was pills.

I told her kid gloves wouldn't help.

She wished I'd watch what I said around the children.

"I'm not about to keep my opinions bottled up," I said. "They know when you're not being straight with them."

"Yes, but *listen* to yourself. Always so negative. Never trusting anyone, railing about the town—"

I laughed. "This from the woman who's out singing at the Test Site every night?"

She nodded. "I know. I just think . . . I worry that maybe we've given him a bleak view of life."

"His views are his own," I said. "He's a smart boy. Besides, I don't see a whole lot to stand up and cheer about here in Tilton, do you?"

She didn't answer me.

"Well, do you?" I said.

She started to cry. I apologized and wrapped my arms around her. "Please," I whispered. "I didn't mean it." I slid my hands to her waist and began to rock with her, gently. Just then I noticed Dana, standing in the kitchen doorway, watching us through tears.

"Dana? Baby, what is it?" I said, squeezing Peg.

"You said you were happy," she told me. "As long as Mom and Scott and me were here. You said so, Dad."

"I am, sweetie. I *am* happy," I said.

"Then why were you yelling at Mom? Why is Mom so sad?"

Peg knelt to hug her. She told Dana she wasn't really sad— "It's just that we're all so tired right now."

Dana wiped her face. "Oh. Have we all been tired for a long, long time?"

I was prepared to skip the football game, to cook a special meal for Peg and the kids. Bouillabaisse? *Enchiladas suizas?* Or maybe something simple, Dana's favorite, jalapeño corn bread.

Peg said no. I could feel her exhaustion, like heat. "The major's important," she said. "Maybe he *can* help us somehow. Go, go. And try to have a good time."

The nights were unusually cool now; I wrapped a sweater around my shoulders.

Downtown, chubby men with baseball caps and flashlights were guiding drivers into narrow parking slots. The stadium rose like a pallid mountain out of the desert, frozen in powdery light from steel towers behind the bleachers.

I stood in line behind a turnstile, gripping my ticket. I watched the Cougar fans—my community, the people I'd pledged to serve. They were boisterous and loud. They smelled of sweet cologne, sweat, and wet socks. Sticky spit-out gum slowed our feet.

Soldiers, miners, engineers; men stooped from their jobs and from family demands; men who lived for Friday-night football—the damaging grace of boys' bodies slamming one another into the grass. I'd seen fellows like these in Texas. Worn-out guys thickened by repetitive labors, leathered by the sun, reduced to an early, beer-bellied dotage. They were fawned over by their grandchildren at family reunions, numbed by mounds of potato salad, left to stew in their juices—Red Man, Skoal—while their wives took care of kids, dogs, food: the important business of life.

Lynn called to me from a garish concession stand. We bought chili dogs and Pepsis and found our place in the bleachers. The Tilton High Cougars took the field, gleaming in golden helmets. They shoved each other's shoulders, warming up. They ran in place. Stark precision. The crowd chanted, "Ooh! Ooh! Ooh!" as though having dry heaves.

Salvation and sacrifice; "Visitors" and "Home"; zero to zero. The future lay ahead.

Raptly, every voice in the stadium sang the national anthem. Then the game began and people splintered into talk groups, catching up on the latest, ignoring the onfield action. I overheard two insurance men discussing car wrecks. They seemed excited and stunned by the terrible facts of their jobs. There was only one woman in our section. She held a shapeless baby in a blanket, a lump of sodden infancy. Below us, the *thwacks* of players' helmets sounded like train cars colliding.

The Cougars completed a pass to midfield. The crowd settled in and began to concentrate on the game.

Lynn said, "Looking Glass." He unwrapped his food.

"Sorry?"

"What you saw the other night. The noise, the wings. If you really want to know . . . I shouldn't be telling you, but I want you to trust me, Jon. It was Looking Glass."

This statement left me blank.

"Strategic Air Command," he explained. He wiped his hands on a napkin. "It's an EC-135—essentially a Boeing 707, modified for greater maneuvering capability." For the last thirty years, he said, a Looking Glass plane had patrolled the skies day and night in case America's ground-based missiles were knocked out in a nuclear attack. "If our bunker people were rendered inoperable by a BOOB—"

"Excuse me?" I said.

"A Bolt out of the Blue. Then Looking Glass has the power to retaliate."

"You mean . . . to launch a nuclear war?"

"At the President's go-ahead, of course." He said the Looking Glass pilot always wore a patch over one eye, to protect it from atomic light. The plane's internal air system could block fallout for thirty-six hours.

"But if everyone's dead on the ground, eventually it'll run out of fuel, right?" I said.

"That's correct." He looked at me as though this bit of common sense were a military secret. Recent defense cutbacks had grounded Looking Glass, he told me. "She only flies occasionally now, at random." This saddened him.

On the field a player was down. He clutched his left knee and writhed in the muddy yellow grass. Lynn stood. "What's happened?" he said.

"I don't know. Looks like our quarterback's been rendered inoperable."

For a moment no one moved on the field. The officials and coaches seemed paralyzed. The linemen stood around like big mistakes.

"Major, what's the Jack Dempsey?" I asked.

He looked at me. "Lynn," he said. "Lynn Lynn Lynn."

"Lynn. Right. Some hush-hush project?"

He sat back down. "What does this have to do with your concerns? 'Sharing ideas,' as I remember—"

"I saw a sign."

"Jon, don't get caught up in intrigue, okay? Life here isn't a spy novel." He finished his dog. We watched a few plays in silence. Then he turned to me. He said in the last decade or so Nevada had been booming—no pun intended. "When Reagan announced his Star Wars plans back in the eighties, every aerospace corporation in the country came here hoping to squeeze cash like water out of our cacti—and the real estate developers weren't far behind. All those boys who'd been building megamalls in California zipped out here in their Porsches and Mercedeses, buying up land to sell to every wanna-be laser-maker—because we already had the base here, see? Same thing happened in Colorado, Wyoming, Utah—everywhere the government had a nuclear stake. This is all public knowledge. People thought they'd get rich. Some did. Whole towns blossomed. Airports were built."

He bought us a couple more Pepsis from a passing vendor.

"But then the Soviet Union went broke, the wall came down in Berlin, our own national debt shot up, wagging its goddam head like a fucking hard-on out of control, all the S&Ls fell apart—they'd fattened up most of the Star Wars research here. The President cut the defense budget. Poof. A lot of your instant millionaires disappeared. Hundreds of fly-by-night projects—developmental things, fledgling companies hoping to do business with the military—faded into the dust. That sign you saw. What was it?"

" 'The Jack Dempsey,' it said."

"I suspect it was some little outfit that fell victim to the local economy. That's all."

I told him the sign looked too official for that. "Besides, what would the Abel Oil Corporation have to do with it?"

The Cougars kicked a field goal. The boy cheerleaders tossed their female partners spinning into the air.

"First it was ranching. Then it was oil," Lynn said. "Now split atoms are the lifeblood of the West. The smart boys in petroleum probably hopped into bed with as many nuclear-power brokers as they could—I would have."

I asked him then, if defense had been cut and the local economy was reeling, why the Test Site seemed as active—maybe even more so—than ever. If the nuclear threat had diminished, why resume atmospheric testing?

Instead of answering he waved at the field. For the first time I noticed that several of Tilton's players were black or Hispanic. I'd only seen whites on the streets.

"We've got a special place here," Lynn said. "And some of us are determined to protect it. Where would those boys and their families be if the defense industry shut down hereabouts? Add to them all the old NASA folks who came our way when the agency hit hard times. They're selling insurance, cars, real estate. Remember Frank Borman—famous astronaut? He's pushing Hyundais now in Las Cruces, New Mexico. You wouldn't begrudge him a chance to make a living, would you?

"Besides, Jon, we're the planet's only remaining superpower, and we want to keep it that way. Germany and Japan mustn't be allowed to challenge us. We have to stop the spread of nuclear know-how to Third World nations. There are scads of reasons for the United States to maintain regular tests. Just because the tension's eased a bit right now, that's no reason to go soft."

The Cougars scored again. We didn't speak for a while. I noticed a boy about Scott's age laughing and kissing a girl a few rows away, in the bleachers. Scott was probably brooding in his bed at home, or giving Peg fits. He should be here, I thought. He should be kissing a pretty girl. He shouldn't have a care in the world.

At halftime Lynn asked to see my budget. I showed him a line-item list. He nodded and said it was doable. He asked again if he could escort me through the DOE's western facilities. My plays were scheduled next month—if the theater was ready. "After that, then," Lynn said. "We'll take a week and I'll show you what we're really all about."

As the second half began, the clouds cleared. The teams' practice formations matched the constellations. A Great Square in the

Cougar backfield collapsed into a Dipper-shaped bump-and-run over the middle.

The opposing team took the opening kickoff. The receiver cut through his blockers' wedge and sprinted up the right hash-mark. The Tilton High players trailed him like a swarm of bees. The receiver lifted his knees as he ran. He held the ball as if it were a breast. He looked as if he'd never stop, as if he'd run through a bleacher exit into the streets, by the muddy buses parked there, on into the desert, past the dinosaur tracks and ca-liche pits, the all-night casinos and hourly-rate motels, the taco stands and gas station restrooms smelling of aftershave, sexual van-ity, panic, sweat, and piss, then onto the tarred and oily backroads whose only reason for being was the desperate need to leave a desperate place, over the Sierra Nevadas, under swooping hawks and eagles, deep into California's redwood forests, through ferns and matted underbrush, farmer's fields, the Silicon Valley, all the way to the coast where America tumbles off a cliff, where America comes to an end.

THAT NIGHT after the game my sleep was ragged. Scott's moods; the theater's troubles; night-rumbles . . .

The Strategic Air Command, for God's sake.

At one point, early in the morning, I dreamed of an old "Don't Litter" ad I'd seen on TV as a child. The ad featured a rugged Indian in a buckskin jacket standing by a superhighway. A car passed. One of its occupants tossed garbage at the man's moccasined feet. A tear ran down his cheek. His face was X'ed with deep, shaded lines, like little riverbeds.

Then the dream shifted to eastern Arizona and the girls we'd seen selling candies and balls by the road. They came to me offering colored confections. "*Manju, manju,*" they said, but they were hard to hear over a grinding roar in the earth. Suddenly the ground at our feet cracked. The girls vanished in roiling smoke. I coughed, wiped my eyes. Out of nowhere the girls appeared again, but now their hands were empty, thrust toward me, begging for cash. Their skin was blackened with ash; hair fell in patches from their heads. They sang quietly of hope and devastation.

I woke, sweating. Peg and the kids were deeply asleep. I stepped outside to smoke a cigarette and to jab the punching bag a little. A light breeze moved through the sage. Moonlight like fiery water filled the dinosaur track.

This landscape was starting to haunt me. My family has always yielded to ghostly memories. All our lives we refute them or repeat them, trying to come to terms with what we've learned.

Like my mother. I knew where her oil field woman came from. I'd heard the story in her kitchen years ago when I was twelve. Dad probably knew it, too, though we'd never discussed it. In those days, when I was a kid, Mother suspected my older sister was in trouble, smoking dope, driving into dark fields with boys in dirty pants. "When I was her age I could've wound up that way," Mom said. "It would've been easy. Now your sister."

"What way do you mean?" I asked.

She told me the story then. I've never forgotten it. Even now I can repeat it word for word, just the way she spoke it.

"When she was young, my mother—your Grandma June—was very beautiful. My father's a fortunate man to've touched her," Mom began. In my mind her voice is always strong and young. "He was an oil worker in the East Texas fields, and not too smart, not too good or bad. At Christmas he drove home to Dallas, bringing us store-wrapped gifts, and slept with us in the house. Your grandmother kept him busy with the vegetables for dinner or the furnace or anything else that needed looking after. At night he combed her blond hair and when he got through his hands seemed to take on her fair color and not the deep black they always seemed to be. But that's me, you know, because I know his hands weren't black. He washed the oil off—I never even saw crude oil—but he worked in the fields and I see him now, dark, in my mind.

"The woman who took him from us wasn't beautiful like your grandmother but she slept in the shanties by the fields and sooner or later he found her, like they all did I suppose, all the men who worked the East Texas fields. It wasn't uncommon to see women strapping on their shoes at night and heading for the fields, because there was money to make and they knew it. So he found her sooner or later. If he came home at Christmas he didn't work around the house anymore. Then he didn't come at all and he was with her, we knew. My brother Bud was old enough to take care of us now, so he said, 'Don't worry,' but I knew he'd be lost, like Daddy. The fields were the only place for him to go."

One night, driving home for the weekend, Bud ran his car off the road two miles south of a rig he'd been roughnecking. He never regained consciousness, Mother said.

"Did he ever see your father?" I asked her.

"No, and he didn't meet a woman of his own. He wasn't the type to take up with that sort, and anyway we'd heard the shanty woman was dead by now, killed by some old boy who didn't want to pay for her. They found her half-burned in the Mayberry Field, dress off, doused with gas."

"Whatever happened to Grandpa?" I asked.

"We heard about him, sick and dying, in a Kilgore clinic years later." My mother rubbed her throat; she'd gone dry. As in many family stories, the initial point had been lost in the telling. I never understood her fear about becoming the kind of woman she'd described. Maybe she'd been tempted to follow the oil workers herself when she was young, to raise money for June, who'd had to scramble for cash after Grandpa disappeared. In fact, my mother didn't leave home until she met my father—who also eventually wound up in the fields.

(My sister, more level-headed than Mother ever gave her credit for being, turned out fine. She's married now and living in Atlanta.)

That night, over twenty years ago, sitting with me in her kitchen, my mother laughed sadly. She told me—smoking here in the desert, I've remembered again—"I don't know what's so damned attractive about the oil fields, but every man in my life —my father, my brother, your dad—has been drawn to them."

I remember thinking, Not me. Something better lies ahead. I won't be trapped by that hard-packed Texas ground.

"Bud was such a good kid," she said. "There was no need for it, no need for it at all. . . . When he ran his car off the road, people said the marks looked like he'd swerved to miss something, but there weren't any tracks in the dirt."

At twelve, I was already familiar enough with her grim tales to know they usually ended with guilt or remorse. I knew what Bud had swerved to miss on the road that night. I knew why Mother worried about my father when he worked late. The oil field woman would haunt my family from now on.

My father's always been a quiet man, and shy, and even if the shanties still stood during his wildcatting days he wouldn't have gone to them for the world. But the Mayberry Woman, as she was known in the fields, came to the oil workers now, the way she'd come to Bud and stood like fog in the middle of the road. She didn't say why she came. Maybe she was looking for her money, though what could it mean to her now?

In 1963 my father moved up in the small oil company he worked for. He stopped going to the fields. He bought an air conditioner and a new car for us and paid off the mortgage on June's Dallas home. In the evenings we watched television: I recall early, grainy footage of Vietnam, before the U.S. ground troops arrived. The Kennedy assassination. Oswald and Ruby. No one told me stories at night to put me to bed. My mother fretted about my sister, my father read the paper. In time I began to realize it was up to me: I'd been given a version of a story, though I was too young to know how to tell it.

For a long time the story stayed inside me. When I was a little older (but still too young to know how to begin) I scared myself with it. Watching meteors one dusk in a mesquite-ridden field I had the sense that the Mayberry Woman was just behind a bush. I wouldn't go to her. A few yards away, on the highway, diesel trucks signaled one another with their horns. I hoped she'd know the drivers were stronger men than I was, full of hard little pills to keep them awake. They'd give her more of whatever it was she was looking for than I could. Presently a jeep loaded with Mexican boys pulled up to the edge of the field. The sky had turned coal-black. A spotlight in the back of the jeep flashed on and the boys fired at cottontail rabbits cowering in the mesquite. I sank into myself. The shots didn't come my way. As they hunted, the boys sang a story of their own:

> La pena y la que no es pena; ay llorona
> Todo es pena para mí.

The story was similar to mine: an airy woman, damp with sweat and talcum and cheap perfume, walked the streets of a Mexican town, touching the faces of children, seducing men from the taverns, lying with them in the backseats of rusted cars.

The hunters laughed and didn't even want the dead rabbits. I imagined that, years from now, after they'd forgotten this night, they'd remember the story they were singing. "La Llorona" was more embedded in their minds than the spotlight and the guns, and I felt a kind of kinship with them.

Now my mother sees the oil field woman everywhere she looks —in her room at the retirement home, in the lobby there, in the john. She has a story to understand—her father's betrayal of her mother—and she can't quite grasp it. It's the torment of her life.

Last week when I phoned Dad he said she hadn't changed. She still thinks *he* had a fling with the family ghost. The other night he'd found her sitting up in bed, in the near-dark, twining yarn. From the big-screen TV in the lobby, canned laughter echoed down the hall. The curtains in Mother's room rustled with the air vent. Dad said she was squinting, trying to catch the movement. "That whore is there at the window," she told him. "She's laughing at me. Listen. Why do you let her go on? Stop her! Goddammit, Frank, tell her to stop!"

He's taken to sleeping on a cot in her room each night.

And me—most dusks I sit in a lawn chair outside the trailer, facing the dinosaur track, smoking cigarettes. I'm haunted, too. I wait for blasts to rip the sky or sleek metal crafts to crash through rocks.

High-tech spirits.

My parents' fears seem quaint as old postcards to me. Mom and Dad have only an inkling of the world *my* family knows.

Years ago, on certain pine-scented Oregon evenings, I felt I still belonged to my parents' world, a simple world that always made sense—though it didn't, really, not all the time. Peg and I often argued about whose turn it was to stay with the baby while the other took a break. In those early days, before we adjusted our bodily rhythms to Scott's, the house would get so tense I'd leave and walk among the darkened fir trees in the hills behind our lot—they appeared to be giant tufts of hair; they made a sound, in wind, like applause. Cheering the night. The warm, safe lights of our rooms.

Overhead, starlight, brilliant, except when bird shadows creased the sky, blotting out for a moment the Scorpion, the Lion, the Lyre: juncos heading home for the evening; squawking jays, as vain as they were loud, seeking night ponds in which to preen their puffy chests. I remember Peg scolding me once for telling Scottie that Steller's jays wore soft, dark clitorises on their heads. But it's true. That's what their feathers looked like.

OUR TOWN turned out to be a modest success. The theater wasn't perfect. The stage was still warped (the actors—all locals—were warned), but we'd finally straightened most of the seats and the space wasn't bad.

I Xeroxed dozens of fliers and posters, ran a couple of ads in the paper, and drew, for the single performance, SRO. It took three separate conversations for me to convince Lynn that he wasn't the right "physical type" for the part of the Stage Manager (this was a dodge). I mollified him by letting him give a brief introduction, inaugurating the theater. He called this opening night our "test flight, our maiden thespian voyage" and left the stage waving both his thumbs. Afterward he confided to me that addressing a theater crowd in a darkened room wasn't the same as barking at a bunch of green recruits under blistering sunlight —"I was actually a little nervous up there"—and that maybe he needed a bit more practice before he tried out for any more parts. No actor myself, I managed to suggest to him that this would be Tilton's enduring loss.

In the days following the performance I received a number of encouraging notes from town officials ("Two thumbs up!" wrote General Thompson). Heartened, I set my Beckett plans in motion. I'd earned the community's trust. They'd learned that the arts wouldn't kill them. Beckett was a far cry from Thornton Wilder, but I'd paved the way for a little adventurousness. After all, *Our Town* wasn't a completely traditional play. It had an unconventional structure and "dead" characters talking up a storm, but Tilton had responded positively. This place could handle Beckett, I told myself. And if it couldn't . . . well, I needed to test its sophistication. Was anyone here my spiritual kin? My maiden voyage had suggested a successful campaign.

The night before Beckett I was locking the theater's back entrance, on my way home, when I spotted a Vietnamese woman sweeping the sidewalk beside a 7-Eleven. Three or four Vietnamese families ran stores in and around Tilton.

The streets were filled with children chasing late-season fireflies. The kids cupped their palms, trapping the bugs, making sharp roofs out of their fingers. Lights glowed inside the tiny homes of their hands.

An old B-52, followed by two olive-green cargo planes, hustled overhead on its way to the Site, warming the street-level breeze. The sweeping woman stopped. How often had she heard these planes threatening her city or village? I wondered. How did she feel now, seeing them every day, their power reduced to the dull tack of training routines?

She caught me watching her. Politely, she bowed.

I was touched by the hard dignity in her face. I bowed to her, a vague gesture of empathy, grief?

She bowed again. I bowed again, deeper.

For *Godot*'s opening night (I planned a two-week run) I'd hung a series of full-color Jackson Pollock prints on the tan brick walls of the theater. Like Jack Dempsey, Pollock was a child of the West—he was born in Cody, Wyoming—and became a national icon. A scowling cowboy with a quick-draw paintbrush. In the forties he'd posed for a *Life* magazine cover wearing a dark jacket, puffing a cigarette. He looked as if he'd just escaped *The Grapes of Wrath*: a pure-blooded, all-American existentialist-tough guy, lovable, irascibly charming, reminiscent of young Hemingway.

Behind him, an ominous black canvas—an abstract flash—announced a powerful new force in the culture.

Critics speak of his violence, but several of his images are gentle and nostalgic—elegies for the bright, swirling spaces he knew as a boy. *Autumn Rhythm, Number 30*, one of the prints I featured, looks more like a soft prairie dust storm than a New York fall. *Wooden Horse, Number 10A*, with its shiny red surface, is as solid and sensual as a saddle.

Jimmy, my director friend, added sagebrush and sand to Beckett's spare set.

Soft blue lighting streaked the gym's rough walls; to dampen the stale athletic smell we burned incense—jasmine and rose. As the audience took its seats I played a taped recording of John Cage's Concerto for Prepared Piano and Chamber Orchestra. Its random time set the mood for the play. Peg had warned me, "These people have very simple tastes, Jon. You don't want to overwhelm them."

"They'll love it," I said. "Don't underestimate them just because most of them have never been to Manhattan. That's a very elitist view."

"You're staging Samuel Beckett in an army town, and *I'm* elitist?" She smiled and kissed me. "You love being provocative, don't you?"

"Look how well they did with Wilder. This'll be even better. They've never experienced anything like this. They'll talk about it the rest of their lives."

"As I said, Jon, you love to provoke. And *I* love you for it. Good luck tonight."

Military regalia looked incongruous in the theater. Lynn waved to me from the front row. None of the black or Hispanic families from the football game had come. A number of the civilians wore string ties and snakeskin boots, fringed blouses. As I watched them I felt nervous for the first time—maybe I *should* have toned things down. I remembered an afternoon, years ago, in Houston's Menil Museum. I was studying a Magritte painting of a woman's face merged with a naked torso (breasts for eyes, puckered vagina for mouth) when two loud women in muumuus paused to look. They were shocked and confused. I tried to be polite, to ease their discomfort. "It's called *The Rape*," I said. "Do you suppose he titled it after he'd painted it, or do you think he had the title in mind first?"

They glared at me as though I'd grabbed them. "She," the louder woman said. "Not he, young man, it's *she*. René. René Mar-ga-reet."

Now, as the last of the ticket-holders filed into the hall, I imagined an audience full of those women.

As soon as the play began, my stomach dove for the floor. I should have listened to Peg. I *did* like to challenge viewers, but in this case their hatred was much worse than I'd anticipated, harsher than any I'd ever seen. A third of them walked out during Lucky's long speech. (The actors were good, I thought, and Jimmy's direction expert.)

I stood in the back, in a dark corner, sweating and panicked. My heart began to ache. The sweet, drifting incense sickened me.

Didi and Gogo wondered if they should hang themselves from the tree. Someone shouted, "For God's sakes, yes! Get this damn thing over with!"

The last twenty minutes were disastrous. Yelling, booing, loud fake retching.

Zack and Beth Heron bravely stayed till curtain. They congratulated me, wanly, on their way out. "I didn't understand a lick of it," Beth said, "but I figure the writer knows what he's talking about."

Zack was pale. He denied that the play had upset him. "It's the damn flu or something," he said. "Been hanging on for weeks. Anyways, Jon, thanks for your show."

"Thank *you* for coming."

The rest of the crowd left shouting and angry.

Afterward I told Peg, "What do these people want? Velvet

paintings of Jesus, cheap wind-up toys, *The Sound of* fucking *Music*?"

"You know what they want. That's why you started with *Our Town*. You just rushed things this time, that's all." She warned me that success in Tilton would depend on accommodating the public, at least in part. "You'll have to educate them slowly. They're not used to real art, Jon. Besides, this was just one night."

" 'I shall rush out as I am,' " I said, remembering *The Waste Land*, " 'and walk the street with my hair down. . . .' "

"Give them another chance, okay? They'll come around. How could they not?"

The following morning, Chick and Tommie crept around the office as if sneaking through a morgue.

"What what *what*?" I said finally.

Tommie showed me a newspaper. "Beckett in the Desert," it said. "Don't Bother 'Waiting' in Line." The reviewer called *Godot* an "obscure affront to common sense" with "gibberish instead of dialogue." The Pollocks, he said, were "child's play without the naive charm of youth." In sum, he wrote, a "dismal setback for our new arts czar, after the hopeful beginning of his initial production."

"Where the hell does this guy get off calling Beckett 'gibberish'?" I said.

Chick mumbled, "Sorry, sir."

"Chick!"

"Right. Sorry, Jon."

The review's byline said "Harper Hardwick." I went looking for him. The *Tilton Examiner* was located next to "Grandma's Downtown Bakery" and a phone booth whose phone was always ringing. No one ever answered it. A cardboard sign in Grandma's window said, "Hot Tarts, 39 cents."

Harper Hardwick was a wiry little man. He was too old to be wearing his Elvis sideburns. Before he even knew who I was I let him have it. It's one thing to critique a performance or the overall quality of a production, I said, but it's asinine to attack Beckett and Pollock. Their reputations as innovative artists were established long ago; surely we're past the point of arguing their merits. "For Christ's sake, grow up," I told the man. "The twentieth century's nearly over and you've fucking missed it."

Hardwick stood, tugging at his belt buckle—a silver medallion embossed with the gold word "Hoss."

"Gertrude Stein," he said.

"What's that?"

"America's the oldest country in the world for anticipating the twentieth century earlier than anyone else."

It was a crude paraphrase, but I knew the Stein quote he meant.

"I'm not some country bumpkin, Mr. Chase. I know who Samuel Beckett is."

"Then why—"

"Because I don't have a choice." He told me his reviews were carefully scrutinized not just by the paper's managing editor but by top army brass, to ensure their wholesomeness, their support of community values. Personally, he'd enjoyed the production, he said, though he thought the actor playing Didi was too strident. He assured me the town wanted me to succeed, but local leaders didn't like the "progressive" direction I'd indicated. They wanted patriotic art, art that promoted family, home, Christian worship, service to the nation. Simple, straightforward, "realistic" art, he said.

"I'm surprised you didn't know what you were letting yourself in for," he added. "It doesn't take a genius to see what this place is all about."

"I got snared in my own enthusiasm," I admitted. "So what're you telling me—your views are censored?"

He tapped his fingers on his desk, glanced to see if his colleagues were listening. "They never say 'censored.' They 'strongly suggest.' I don't want to jeopardize my job, Mr. Chase."

I shook my head.

He held out his hand. "Lubbock," he said.

"Really? I'm from Midland." We shook.

"I know. Practically neighbors. I lived in West Texas all my life until I got drafted."

He poured us both black coffee. His advice: cut my losses, cancel the production. Stage *Heidi* or something like that.

He was right. The rest of the week, the theater was nearly empty. After only three performances we were over eight hundred bucks in the hole.

Scott sat in the front row each night, howling with laughter and delight.

LATE ONE SATURDAY NIGHT, Jimmy and his crew flew, grumbling, back to Texas. After only five performances I'd ditched the play. I was angered and hurt by the whole affair, but Peg and I had agreed, for the kids' sake, to display only optimism, bright as the yellow nasturtiums she'd bought for the trailer; my frustrations were reserved for the punching bag at midnight when everyone was asleep.

I'd quit smoking, not easily. My upper body was stronger now, still fluid but hard. I'd discovered Time in my muscles—the weight of each passing second when your arms wear out, the dream of a never-ending present as long as you're locked in a rhythm. As soon as you stop, your body seems to age. It shivers. Sags. Falls out of Time, into an inert, fading world like boxers in scratchy old film reels knocked to the canvas, useless and dead as rocks.

Peg had always told me that pain is the muscle and bone of grace. Early in her career, she'd studied testimonies of torture victims. "They're my distant kin," she said. "Like dancers, they're forced to live in their physical selves more keenly than most folks." Electrodes and whips aren't the worst punishments, she told me. "Cruelty is when you're made to stand without moving. After an hour you start to hate your arms, your legs and feet. The adult skeleton puts an enormous amount of pressure on itself."

My moonlit workouts were beginning to show me what she'd meant all these years.

Week after week my stamina was improving, but I still couldn't whack the bag more than thirty minutes at a time. After a last flurry I'd fall into a lawn chair, let my sweat massage me. The desert moved or didn't, depending on the breeze. Some nights my thoughts jumped from the sweet science to the art of knowing the world. I wondered if I were a painter how I'd capture this land. First of all it's broken, I noticed one night. Everywhere: shattered. Cracked rocks, split sticks, bitten ridges, branches, ravines. Dry promises of freedom, air and light. No focal point—stubbornness, intransigence. A refusal to be revealed. It's an unpaintable landscape, finally. An artist might go for the sand, the various shades of sunset. But where's the *meaning* in an image like that? Meaning lives in the foreground, I thought, not the setting—or in the interplay between the two, like a pair of boxers squaring off, dodging, weaving, lashing out at their own weaknesses, embodied in their fleshy opponents.

One evening when Peg was at the Site and the kids were taking their showers, Harper Hardwick pulled up in a red Ford Mercury. He held a six-pack in a sack. "Hoped you wouldn't mind a visit," he said.

With my foot I shoved a lawn chair over in his direction. He twisted the caps off a couple of bottles and handed me a lukewarm Bud.

"Sorry about your play," he said, in that Texas/Southern way of slowly warming up a conversation.

"Well, you warned me," I said.

He gave my punching bag a nod. "You box?"

"Only for exercise. What's on your mind?"

He popped a finger into his bottle, then out again. "Something's going on over there," he said, almost reverently. He fingered the air, toward the Test Site. It seemed he was about to trust me—a near stranger—with something important. I figured more questions would spook him, so I sat quietly and let him pace himself.

Long silence. A noisy suck of beer. "Last fall the President said the U.S. was going to scrap over three thousand tactical nukes," he said. "You might've read about it. Lance missiles, antisub bombs, artillery shells, lots of short-range stuff."

I nodded.

"Well, right away I set to work researching a story—which the paper never ran—on how the army defuses all that. It's easy for some politico to say, 'Do away with these things,' but who actually does it, and how do they go about it?"

"Good question," I said.

"With most bombs, you pull the wiring from the tritium canister which holds the helium, deuterium, uranium, and lithium atoms—all the stuff, you know, that makes the big bang."

So he'd gathered impressive facts prepping his story. Why was he so eager to establish his credentials with me?

"But if that's all you do, the thing still works," he said. "Someone could plug it back in at a moment's notice. To honestly kill a bomb, you've got to drain its chemicals, but then what do you do with the waste? You can't leave it lying around; if you ship it somewhere you're vulnerable to terrorist hijacks. Something else I found: the uranium in most warheads is too concentrated to be dumped into nuclear power reactors. So there you are." He sipped his beer. "When I learned all that, I realized this talk of military cutbacks was bullshit," he said. "A shift in priorities, maybe. Defense factory layoffs, maybe. But they aren't really going to destroy these weapons." He glanced at me. "You've heard the blasts?"

"Yes," I said. "They've resumed atmospheric testing."

"With absolute arrogance," Harper added. "I mean, there must be seismic evidence somewhere, but no one's come forward with it. No one's blown the whistle on them. There's as much activity at the Site right now as there ever was in wartime—just the opposite of cutbacks. My guess is, these aren't just conventional tests. They're working on something special."

I reached for another beer. "Why are you telling *me* all this?" I said.

"You know about the Dempsey."

My neck tensed. I shook my head.

He said he'd overheard General Thompson and Lynn talking about me in the diner this morning. They were disturbed by what I'd seen. "So what do you know?" Harper said.

"Nothing. I saw a sign, that's all. Donaldson told me it was some business that'd gone belly up."

Harper said the Dempsey, whatever it was, might be the Test Site's major project now. He wanted to find out. I remembered Lynn's warning me off intrigue. Besides, I told Harper, if he couldn't review a play the way he wanted, why did he think the paper would publish something like this—assuming he learned anything?

"I won't take it to the *Examiner*," he said. "I mean, I don't see myself rotting away here in Tilton the rest of my life. Do you? I've eaten enough dust. If I broke a story with national impact, I could get the hell out of here while I still have my health, *comprende*?"

A dream made in Hollywood—handsome heroes sifting the sands of justice. Redford and Newman. Or maybe Clint Eastwood. The Big Discovery in the Desert.

The idea seemed desperate to me, but perhaps no more so than trying to bring High Culture to a military outpost.

"What brought a smart guy like you here in the first place?" I asked. "And why were they crazy enough to hire you?"

He laughed. "Same as you, I imagine. The need for legal tender. I can be a real good actor when I need a job, but in my line it's hard to end up where you want to be."

"I hear you."

"That's why this is an important story for me. Will you show me the sign?"

"I don't know," I said. "Will you lighten your reviews?"

He smiled. "I'll do what I can."

I said, "Tomorrow night, then."

Dismantling Beckett. I tossed the tree out back, into a dirt pit behind the gym. The sadness of the moment echoed earlier losses in my life; as I sat on the sand in the dark converted playhouse, I pictured the West Texas dunes where I first fell in love—*my most important discovery in the desert*. I was sixteen. The girl's name was Linda. I stared at the empty seats and remembered.

My father had lent me his car for the evening. I'd driven out Highway 80 by the Odessa Meteor Crater (even then it was going to seed; only a Dr Pepper sign marked its access road), past an X-rated drive-in picture screen angled toward the highway. Linda and I saw a naked thigh the size of a gas truck. She told me to pull over next to a railroad trestle. A refinery hissed in the distance. Smoke, thick as mattress stuffing, hung in the air.

Linda scrambled over the trestle gripping a paper cup. She wanted to pick dewberries. Black, purple, and red, they looked like little clusters of grapes. Their juice smoothed our lips, sweetened our quick, shy kisses. A jet moved overhead and a sudden warm wind shook the mesquite.

By the time we reached the dunes the entrance gate was locked. We climbed the wire mesh fence, spilling our berries, then leaped ankle-deep into the sand. Linda ran, leaving birdlike tracks. She whooped. The sand was cool. We rolled down the hills and once, when we stopped, we stripped and made love. I don't know how long we lay there together, but when I looked up again the stars had moved.

Time disappeared. Right then I knew only the intensity of the young body beside me, and my own pale body, trembling with excitement. Lovely Linda. I hadn't thought of her in years —we'd lost track of each other after high school. As I sat there imagining her with me in Beckett's dim world, her features sifted into Peg's, and a more recent memory took shape.

That very morning Peg had told me she was pregnant again. We hadn't planned another child. Neither of us knew what to feel, and we didn't talk about it before I left for work.

Now, hours later, I still didn't know what to think. I remembered when Peg was carrying Dana. After her first morning's visit with the obstetrician she was so excited to tell me what she'd learned. "The doctor says X-X—I'm talking chromosomes—make girls, and X-Y boys," she said. "But apparently all fetuses start X-X. Y's don't do much . . . they're junk chromosomes." She gave me a brief, gene-disparaging glance. "Women don't have them, only men do."

Another night, late in her term. I'd just bought a personal computer for my study. All day I'd been reading Error Messages and Basic Operations Procedures from the instruction manuals. For some reason Peg found the phrases sexy. "The result of the ASC function is a numerical value that is the ASC II code of the first character of the string," I read, and "The *n* argument can be a construct such as 12 or it can be *equal-variable*." She pulled me into bed with her, turned over on her face, and propped herself up with a pillow. "It's more comfortable for me like this," she said.

I kissed the cleft of her back, up and down her spine. "You're incredibly beautiful," I said.

"You like fat women?"

"Generally, no. But you're exquisite. Are your breasts sore?"

"A little. I think it'll be okay if you go easy."

That night, I recall, the house smelled of mushrooms and eggs. We'd eaten in front of the television: a videotape of *City Lights* which I'd rented from a store. Peg had always been a slapstick fan. While watching the Little Tramp she'd placed her hand beneath her tummy as if to weigh it. "Physical comedy," she said.

In bed I moved against her. I hummed a tune from the film.

"In another few weeks it won't be possible to do this," she said. "I'll be too big and it might be bad for the baby."

"Let's go slow then," I told her. "Make it last."

Her pleasure (the way she offered and lost herself so thoroughly) made me beam with delight. Rain crackled on the pine needles in the trees outside our window.

"Any number of statements can be executed at the same time," I whispered in her ear. "Multiple definitions can be in effect for the same rough data."

"Mmmm," Peg said. "What's it mean?"

"I don't know," I said. "Something about the impossible."

"Like making love with a boulder in the bed?"

"Like paying this kiddo's bills for the next twenty years."

Now patterned light—filtered through the theater's dark double windows—scored the stage's wooden floor.

Another baby.

Late nights, spit-up and shit.

Extra laughter in the house.

I stuffed a hat into a prop box and, for the moment, shut the lid on art.

"What we're after is multiplicity. Situations, not scenes."

Peg's voice rose above the trailer. She'd gathered her comrades from the Test Site to practice a few simple dance steps.

"The more precise our aesthetics," she told her friends, "the more incisive our public impact."

Twenty women—adolescent, elderly, in between—surrounded her near the dinosaur track. Some of them wore leotards and warm-up suits. Peg was dressed in a simple white shift with spandex tights. My pregnant wife. She looked happy and enthusiastic with her pupils. I wanted them all to leave so I could be alone with her.

She suggested the group use television to denounce the blasts, to urge passage of the nuclear testing moratorium bill in the U.S. House and Senate. "In order to draw the camera's attention, our movements will have to be fluid," she said.

She told them about Merce Cunningham, her favorite choreographer, how he'd once attempted to convert the daily confusion of urban streets into dance. "He looked for the underlying threads of motion—the hidden recurrences. Now, *our* field of interpretation is the Test Site. The challenge is to translate our emotional pain into physical reality."

The women looked puzzled, but they trusted her. She led them through a series of arm gestures: long, sweeping arcs.

Repetition had become a key element in her work. The body's not solid, like sculpted stone, she'd told me; its closest approach to *permanence* is to repeat itself until certain motions are stored in memory and muscle.

In her last public performance, two years ago in Houston's Griffith Park, she'd illustrated her feelings for the physical by violently clawing at herself—trying to get *inside*—until her thin taffeta dress lay in tatters on the outdoor stage. Nude, she grasped the contours of her rib cage as though she'd pull it apart. Then, like a magician (she *had* taken a couple of lessons, to enhance her act), she unrolled colorful paper scrolls from her ears and mouth. She read from them: mundane descriptions of the park, as if to say what's inside me is nothing more than the sum of my body's experiences. Her tight skin looked like terra-cotta come to life, undulating gently, impossibly, in the hot Texas night. As a finale, she looped and smoothed the scrolls until they formed a rainbow phallus: a transformation from female to male, the body's power to shape and create (digestion, birth, raw physical strength). Her calm and her grace turned a potentially tawdry scene into beauty, joyous and provocative.

Naturally, the mainstream press mocked her or condemned her "pornographic mind," but she stuck by her guns and continued to plan new dances. I knew she'd missed performing.

Now she was helping a Navajo woman named Susie loosen her spine. "That's it," Peg said, raising Susie's arms. "Just let yourself go."

Susie smiled, embarrassed. "I think this is the first thing I've ever done without my husband's permission," she said. She was huge. She wore an orange wraparound dress which left her shoulders bare; a gold tooth shone in her massive brown head. "I feel guilty, a little."

"Forget him," Peg told her. "This is for you. Enjoy yourself."

A forgotten husband (at least for the moment), I ducked inside the trailer. Scott was doing his homework.

"Where's your sister?" I asked.

"She stayed after school for a pep rally or something."

I made myself a sandwich.

"So Mom's going to have a baby?" Scott said.

"That's right. What'll it be? Boy or girl?"

He chewed his pencil. "I'd like a brother."

"Boy it is, then."

Scott hadn't erupted in weeks, and he was doing better in school, but lately he'd developed nervous habits. Whenever he sat, he'd shuffle his feet in a widening circle around his chair, as if clearing space for himself. Sometimes the shuffling lasted twenty minutes or more. When I pointed this out to him, he said he wasn't aware he was doing it. In the last couple of days, he'd added compulsive tapping, rearranging of pencils, erasers, and papers to his weird little dance.

He said he was having restless dreams. Wild, shifting colors. Echoed shouts and screams. Each night he saw a "big hairy man." The same dream, repeated. I asked him who it was. He couldn't see a face. Just a furry figure looming in light and shade.

"Is it a scary dream?"

"Sort of. Not really," he said.

"Will you tell me if your dreams get worse?"

"Sure." He gazed out the window at a dust devil near the horizon. "A baby brother," he said.

"We'll call him Mule. Give him a broom, tell him to sweep the highway every night."

Scott didn't laugh. "He's going to need some damn good survival tips to make it out here," he said.

"Don't we all?"

I squeezed his shoulder. He touched the hanging lamp above

the table, then reached up to touch it again. His feet jerked beneath the chair. I decided to write down his movements. He'd
told me he didn't want to see another doctor, but I knew he'd
have to soon or, like a man falling through space, flailing wildly
at nothing, he'd wear himself out.

I MET HARPER at the diner for a burger and beer before we set off to find the Dempsey. Instinctively we trusted each other —a couple of West Texans—but didn't know if that was smart. Like high school kids on a blind date we asked bold but shy questions and slowly revealed ourselves over dinner. I told him about Scott and about my checkered career. Peg's dancing. He said Vietnam was the central fact of his life.

On R & R in Saigon in '66 he used to hang out at the Butterfly Bar and Grill at the intersection of Tu Do and Tran Hung Dao streets, he said. A tattered French poster for *Love Story* filled the bar's window and he'd go there in the afternoons just to stare at Ali MacGraw's pretty face. Children slept nearby on the sidewalk in front of the Bank of America's gleaming gold doors. GI laughter rocked the Steam Room Massage Parlor. Black marketeers sold Lucky Strikes, Seagram's whiskey, and M-16 ammo rounds. Drunk ARVN soldiers rode in rickshaws carted by scabrous straw-hatted boys.

Every now and then, Harper said, a black Citroën, drilled with tiny holes, swerved into the intersection until it hit a telephone pole or a pedestrian and stopped. Another government official scratched off somebody's list.

"When I got back home I worked as an aide in a public defender's office there in Lubbock," he said. "Our clients were dumb as goats. I'm telling you, the cops couldn't solve half the crimes in this country if it weren't for ignorant people blurting out their secrets. I remember this one guy, he was in jail for robbery and attempted murder. One day he writes a letter to the White House telling Nixon somebody ought to kill him, and 'I'm the man to do it,' he says, 'soon's I get out.' He puts the prison's return address on the envelope, and can't figure out why a pair of FBI goons show up a week later." Harper shook his head. "So I quit. It's hard to defend people like that." He'd been a journalist ever since.

After dinner we hopped into his Mercury and I guided him out of town. All around us the flat fields of Nevada buzzed with busy night bugs.

"Got word from a friend in D.C., says the AP is sending reporters out here to investigate rumors of a hot new spy plane at the Site," Harper said. "His sources at the Pentagon have leaked references to something called Aurora—a jet that can fly four thousand miles per hour and reach altitudes of ninety thousand feet."

He said the Pentagon was furious last year when the government canceled its Blackbird program. For thirty years, these dagger-shaped spy planes had canvassed the world. "Publicly, the Joint Chiefs say without the Blackbird their intelligence capability's fucked," Harper said. "In private, my friend tells me, they've developed 'black programs'—top-secret projects whose funding is disguised in the federal budget as 'selected activities.' What that means is, it's business as usual, though they're telling *us* they've stopped all their testing."

I indicated a side road I'd taken the night the mysterious object sliced around my car. Harper turned. "The mighty Pentagon," he said. "I was there in '67 for the big march. I'd just gotten my discharge from the army." He laughed. "It was wild, man. Naked bodies, painted faces. The building squawked at us through these scratchy damn megaphones—it was like the voices of all our fathers. 'The demonstration in which you are participating ends at midnight. All demonstrators must depart the Pentagon grounds.' I got naked myself—it was irresistible—sang 'God Bless America' and 'We Shall Overcome.' Dancing around out there —I don't know—it felt like such a *liberation* after the war. Heady. Erotic."

A jackrabbit darted through our headlight beam, across deep, dusty ruts.

"Anyway," Harper said, embarrassed by what he'd just told me. "The Aurora. The military denies its existence, of course, but there's plenty of evidence for it." The road got worse. Harper slowed. He said the U.S. Geological Survey in California had finally broken its silence, and reported repeated sonic booms in a path from southern Nevada to California's San Gabriel Valley. Cal Tech seismologists had recently confirmed that some type of aircraft was responsible for the disturbances. The planes appeared to be headed in the direction of Groom Lake, an air force research and development area in the Site. Normally, Harper said, the only thing booming near Groom Lake was a returning space shuttle. San Gabriel Valley residents had complained of cycling, earsplitting shrieks. "Sounds to me like a hybrid rocket-ramjet engine—those babies'd *have* to be on any craft that takes off under its own power and reaches four thousand mph," Harper said.

"I haven't heard anything like that," I told him. "We just get explosions out where I live. You think this Aurora project is related to the sign I saw?"

"Could be. Or could be, in their glee at outlasting the Soviets, they're developing several new things at once."

Moonlight pierced a bank of light clouds. We reached the copper draw. No sign. No evidence of human activity. The breeze carried the creak of an old water-well pump from somewhere miles away. Heat and sand seemed to blend into an entirely new element, attacking all our pores.

"You're sure this is the spot?" Harper said.

"Positive."

"Damn. They probably removed it because of you."

I shivered. I couldn't shake the fear that hidden eyes were on us. "I don't get it. If this is all hush-hush, why would there be a sign in the first place?"

"One thing I've learned over the years: despite their organization and precautions, the military fucks up all the time," Harper said. "Or maybe it was a decoy. Who knows?"

We sat in the dark, disappointed. An owl hooted in a nearby cactus. The air, broiling just moments ago, was cooling fast. Night came in an instant here.

"Wait a minute. I've just realized where we are," Harper said. "This whole area—it used to be part of the Paiute Indian Reservation."

"Used to?"

He nodded. "Uranium was discovered here in the sixties. The DOE moved in and ran the Paiutes off—or put them to work in aerospace factories. There was a big local scandal." Harper switched off his headlights. "The army marched in here one day to chase away the ones who wouldn't leave. People were killed. You'll find the old newspaper accounts in the library morgue. Witnesses said the soldiers raped and murdered over twenty Paiute women. That night back on base, rumor has it, the grunts played catch with a woman's severed breast."

I had no words for this. I nearly choked on my own saliva. Nothing moved except blind white moths tapping the windshield. Harper lighted a cigarette.

How can I bring another child into these salt flats? I thought. I was a child of nowhere myself—the borderless space of the desert—and my son had already inherited the emptiness I'd absorbed.

Better to feel nothing when you're nowhere.

"Are you okay?" Harper said.

"I think so."

"Didn't we leave a couple of beers back at your trailer?"

"Yeah. Let's get out of here."

We sat in my lawn chairs, trying to plan our next move. Just past midnight, the first of many explosions occurred: flashes of green followed by short, shifting trails in the sky.

"Paper and pen," Harper said. "Let's track these suckers."

I made several sketches that night, which I later enhanced with detail, like this:

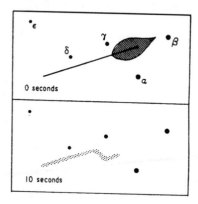 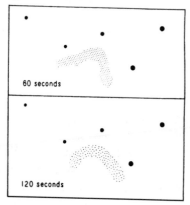

The trails all crossed the same quadrants, near Cassiopeia, and moved in a northeast direction. Each successive blast broke closer to my trailer.

I CONTINUED TO COMPLAIN about the blasts, and to ask about a house, but got shifty answers from Lynn.

As I anticipated, he hated *Godot*. "Next time you'll stage something *on earth?*" he kidded me over coffee one morning in the diner.

That day I happened to have with me a book of European reprints. I showed him a Hermann Otto Hoyer painting of a muscled, square-jawed worker lifting an injured comrade onto his back. Thick blue factory smoke whirled between his boots. The style was strict Soviet Realism.

"Yeah," Lynn said, excited. "Now you're talking. *That's* a work of art. Straightforward, with an actual story behind it."

I told him Hitler had commissioned this painting in '33 as part of a Nazi propaganda campaign.

Lynn frowned. Egg dripped thickly from his fork. "You oughtn't to play tricks on me like that, Jon."

"No tricks," I said. "But how about you order us more coffee?"

"I'm serious, man. Don't be getting sophisticated on me. The thing I like about you, you're a down-to-earth guy. But that play was a dog and you know it."

"It's an acknowledged masterpiece," I said. "Beckett's probably our greatest contemporary playwright."

"I don't care what the so-called experts say. You got to stay grounded, my friend, and give us *real* art, something we can sink our teeth into."

I told him I didn't understand why Tilton had hired me. "Obviously this community wants safe, popular art. Simple diversions. Nothing intellectually challenging," I said. "One glimpse at my résumé and you can see my interest in postmodernism. I'm the wrong man for the job."

Lynn shook his head. "Post-this, post-that—we don't give a hoot, Jon. We—or *me*, I'll speak for myself. Frankly, not everybody *was* keen on hiring you. But right from the start I liked what I saw. Your letter was full of energy and style. I plucked your name right out of the stack of applications. Now, naturally it'll take a while for you to catch the town's rhythms, but you'll get our drift soon enough. I have faith."

I refused to retreat. My next plan was to steer a Rauschenberg show our way. An exhibition of his earliest works, including his first combines (a wooden box tethered to a stone, a metal block glued to mica, pearl, and thread), Zen- and Beat-inspired elemental sculptures, along with his initial experiments in monochrome, was traveling from the Corcoran to the Menil Collection and finally to the San Francisco Museum of Modern Art. I knew it was a long shot—and there was the huge problem of insurance money—but I hoped I could plug into the show as it moved across the country. I drafted quick grant proposals, emphasizing the need to expose out-of-the-way communities to new (or old but poorly disseminated) ideas, like visual abstraction and collage.

"Still hoping to bring the twentieth century to little old Tilton?" Harper asked me one day.

"It's worth a try."

"Believe me, the century's here, Jon. In a big way."

"Its technology is here," I said. "Its heart is conspicuously missing."

I realized now there were at least two agendas—the army's and the public's—I was supposed to fulfill as Tilton's arts commissioner, neither of which matched my own ambitions. Lynn's superiors had taught him to simplify, but grandly: Patriotism, Honor, Courage. To a warrior like him, art was a Noble Celebration of the Human Spirit, as long as it flew the stars and stripes and stayed in safe museums. A soldier's art was classical, with strong narrative compositions and plenty of flowing robes, ladies lifting torches—the Light of Liberty!—or waiting for their lovers in chaste Victorian parlors. A soldier's art was also naive, something delicate to humor and protect, like women and children.

That's why the twentieth century couldn't exist here. Cubism: an art that wrecked the world, then pieced it together again more generously than any conquering army; an art that absorbed large scraps of the daily news. Abstraction: a bold gesture that discarded the world altogether, leaving nothing to justify the use of force. This art was too smart. It wouldn't sit still. It barked all night in its cage.

None of this mattered to the citizens of Tilton. Trapped in harsh jobs with little or no security, they asked to be entertained, they wanted Beauty to wash them like a fresh summer rain: honest expectations, but the packaging wasn't right. If it didn't fit on a postcard or a colorful calendar, if it couldn't be gift-wrapped, it wasn't art in their minds.

"Community values" fell like a net over all these considerations. Nudity was fine for the Christ child but not for anyone else. The pointillists must have had sand in their eyes. "Realism" was the final test of a work, a standard that reduced art to harmless imitation.

Above all, art should never mix with the world. Museums without windows.

I told Harper that, for me, the truest and most moving work is deeply unsure of itself, confused as to whether it's a masterpiece or a heap of junk. Uneasy, trembling with doubt, this is art at its most fallible and human, longing for the world, swallowing in its hunger sheet metal, newspapers, tires, scuffed shoes, or other detritus, drawing the old lives of these things (a touch of wistfulness and nostalgia) into a new life, an altogether different way of being. Renewal, redemption—and of course a critique of life-as-it-is, which is what makes it so threatening.

Ultimately, my disagreements with the people of Tilton weren't just a matter of taste; if that had been the case, none of this would have meant anything. To me it was a question of survival.

If we agreed that sheet metal, newspapers, tires, and scuffed shoes were art, then the world was full of transcendent marvels. Sand and rocks and lizards and old cardboard boxes were extraordinary; perhaps, in certain contexts, even sacred.

If this is how you saw the world—the earth itself a vast museum, a giant open window filled with anxious objects—you wouldn't bomb even the desert.

Could I ever, with limited resources, inspirit these ideas for my neighbors in Tilton? I didn't know.

I ached for my old days in urban spaces, with all their energy, imagination—money. I remembered a wonderful night in Houston, years ago, when Peg was first pregnant with Dana. We'd taken a bottle of sparkling cider to the bayou to watch people float paper lanterns on the water. They were commemorating the bombing of Hiroshima. Wild radishes and fennel grew beside the stream: city salad. I chewed, sipped the cider. Japanese mothers rocked their babies in dark brown prams. It was "Celebrate the Arts" month in Houston: the Chamber of Commerce had established a temporary sculpture garden downtown. Papier-mâché clowns swayed like puppets from the girders of a bridge; a six-foot spider made of Volvo engines crouched beneath a sign.

Smoky lights curled past us on the stream. Delicately crafted, each lantern—a tiny birthday candle wrapped in a paper shell—represented a single human life. They floated erratically down the bayou, bumping abandoned air conditioners, car doors, old refrigerator shelves.

I settled on the grass and untucked Peg's yellow blouse. I

smoothed her belly where our child waited in a place without color. We kissed until the lights went out.

"Are you happy?" Peg asked me one night. The trailer was dark. The kids were asleep.

"Yes." I held her hand.

That morning we'd seen the first ultrasound prints of our baby. Dr. Potts, Peg's obstetrician, spread the images on his office desk for us. All I could see in the pictures was two blurry bars, like a pair of unsharpened pencils, and what appeared to be a series of holes surrounded by rippling waves. The computer-enhanced compositions reminded me of bleak Scandinavian paintings, impressionistic studies of people screaming on rocky, violent seashores.

I pointed to one of the pencils. "Is that a penis?" I asked Potts. "We're going to have a boy?"

"That's the head," he said. His ears were padded with tufts of hair as pale as his papery skin. "I can't be certain, but my guess is you're looking at a lovely little girl."

Peg grinned and squeezed my fingers.

One of her friends at the Site had told her that eight Tilton babies a year were born without brains. Authorities blamed an unknown pollutant in the local air or water. Potts confirmed the terrible figure, but assured Peg she shouldn't worry. "All indications are normal for you," he said.

We'd decided to name the baby Jessie, after Peg's maternal grandmother. The name cheered Peg, but not for long. Her eyes misted, and I knew what she was thinking.

She shivered. I pulled her close. "Let's get our minds off gloomy statistics, all right?" I said. "Let's think of wonderful things. Chili dogs."

Peg smiled. "Jon—"

"Try it, sweetie. Please. For me."

"Okay. Cat fur," she said.

" 'The Potato Head Blues.' Italian ices—"

"Doll's eyes in the dirt." Warmed by a sudden fond memory, she laughed, then settled against my body. "One rainy day when I was twelve my parents left the house—I don't know where they went," she said. Her voice was soft and distant, aimed inward, not at me. "I sneaked one of my father's beers out of the refrigerator. I'd never had a beer. I stuffed it inside this old canvas rucksack of mine and ran down the block. There was a drainage ditch—a round metal pipe—at the far end of the alley behind all the neighborhood houses. I used to crawl in there to hide whenever my folks were mad at me. It was damp, full of little gray frogs. Their croaking echoed in the tunnel. I sat inside the pipe and opened the beer. It was bitter but cold, and I liked that."

I nuzzled her ear.

"Sipping my drink and listening to the frogs, I realized I'd never crawled through the ditch to the other side," she said. "When I finished the beer I dropped the bottle in a puddle and headed for the opposite entrance."

"What did you find?"

"An old abandoned church in an overgrown field. White wooden cross, peeling paint . . . and in the dirt at my feet, empty milk cartons, bottle caps, firework shells—and a pair of doll's eyes. The kind that open and close when you roll them? They were lying, gaze down, in the weeds all by themselves. No sign of the doll. I was delighted—a little dizzy from the beer. I put the eyes in my bag. For the rest of the day—the rest of that week—I felt protected, as though someone were watching me, looking out for my safety. Winking, winking as I walked. . . ."

IN EARLY NOVEMBER, Lynn and I and a helicopter pilot named Moon took a week-long tour of "national security communities" in Wyoming, Colorado, New Mexico. I left Peg my list of Scott's tics and asked her to keep an eye on him.

I didn't know what Lynn wanted. The reasons for this trip were still obscure to me.

Moon flew us in a straight line, north to south, over Casper, Old Fort Laramie, Cheyenne, Boulder, Rocky Flats (newly quarantined by the FBI for illegal storage of radioactive waste), Colorado Springs, Pueblo, Los Alamos, Santa Fe, Albuquerque, White Sands. From the air we followed the oily black spear of Interstate 25 through rolling desert and mountains—Lynn called it the "nuclear highway."

On the ground, in an unmarked military sedan, we followed the same trails the Kiowa Indians had cleared as they stalked dwindling herds of bison, the same paths Coronado had worn, until the feet of his men were bloody, in his search for the Seven Cities of Cibola. We crossed the Sangre de Cristo Mountains, past the rusted remains of a KC-135 tanker jet, downed accidentally in '57; its cargo of hot fuel had gouged a crater in the land twelve feet deep and twenty-five feet wide, Lynn told me, but it only killed a cow.

In the Rocky Mountain foothills we came upon a ghost town.

Scattered in the streets, swim trunks, yo-yos, stereos, deer heads, saddles, a faded American flag. "Defense cutbacks," Lynn said. "This is Tilton soon, if we don't watch out."

At night, our sedan crushed armadillos, paralyzed by the headlights, into thick, steaming meat on the road. Farm reports on the radio. The stock market. I dozed, cracked a window for a wake-up hit of air. Toward dawn, giant yellow numbers—gas prices, beer prices, food prices, all the jacked-up demands of the coming day—swayed on silver poles beside the highway, over wild-onion fields, mint past its prime, poison oak, the leafy cool sump of high country woods.

Though I had no security clearance, Lynn took full responsibility for me at the installations we toured. At the Consolidated Space Operations Center in Colorado Springs, I saw the command post for military space shuttle flights and satellites. At Falcon Air Force Base I saw a war games complex—Lynn told me a series of Cray-2 computers were downlinked to a Los Alamos super-computer to simulate, on a scoreboard, nuclear attacks. "Mega-rad strategic!" yelled a sweating young man, his eyes narrowed on a pink flashing graphic on a screen, while I watched. The military towns were all strip shopping centers and used-car lots, anchored by a few private homes, football stadiums, and the towering steel-and-glass slabs of Honeywell, TRW, Hughes Aircraft, Hewlett-Packard, and IBM.

Back in the desert, Moon driving. Old water heaters twisted across dry rocks. Abandoned couches and recliners, minus their stuffing, trapped blowing trash and sage. Tumbleweeds wrapped the chairs like hungry predators. A billboard ad for Chiquita bananas had lost its grip on a hill; it was sliding, one wooden stake at a time, down the slope.

Every few miles we passed lone ranch houses, television satellite dishes aimed at nothing.

A noisy hot wind shook the car. "Looking Glass," Moon said.

Late that afternoon, at an underground operations center near

Chugwater, Wyoming, Lynn introduced me to a handsome "missileer" named Dan. "Danny boy here was an all-state fullback for the Tilton High Cougars in '89. Now he's one of our silo boys."

Dan grinned—a goofy kid in his early twenties. "Missiles is good for promotions," he told me.

"That's right." Lynn slapped his back. "We take care of our own down in Tilton. What about *your* boy, Jon? He play any sports?"

"No."

"That's a shame."

Dan described his weekly routine. Every twenty-four hours, he said, he and one other person, his "capsule partner," sit in a tiny steel room in a launch control facility underground, monitoring the "health" of MX missiles in their silos. At forty-second intervals, computers electronically ask each missile if it's functioning properly. If it's not, a fault light will signal Dan and his partner. "We get false launch codes all the time," he told me. "Kinks in the system. We have only a few seconds to decide if it's really from the President."

I pictured warheads packed like pistons into thin shafts hidden under acres of harsh prairie grass. The prairie itself looked as battered as the starved fields I'd seen in Nicaragua in '86.

Lynn pointed out another computer, but I couldn't keep my eyes off this smiling puppy, Dan. He had the power to commence the planet's slow burn.

Later, Lynn told me, "We've got a pipeline straight from Tilton into this place—we send 'em our best kids. What else is a guy like Danny going to do? He'll never be a ballplayer, he didn't learn much in school, but here he can be trained, given a shot at self-esteem. That boy's making about thirty-five thou, three years out of high school. If he sticks with the military, chances are when he's out there'll be a sweet job in real estate or auto sales waiting for him—these towns are real proud of their boys. We all look out for them—the blacks and the Mexicans too." He slapped my shoulder. "Good folks, Jon. A family."

"Just like everyone else," I said. "What's the mortgage on a silo?"

He laughed. "Goddam, you're a tough nut to crack. Surely you agree we need national defense?"

"Who'll protect us from *us*?" I knew my terror seemed anachronistic. After all, the Cold War, Mutually Assured Destruction —these were finished issues, right? The President said our children no longer worried about the Bomb. "Something in me refuses to relax," I told Lynn. "Especially when I see all this hardware."

"You're a leftie cynic, raised on the sixties. Naturally it'll take a while for you to let go of those old attitudes." He patted my back. "But believe me, Jon, you'll find it's not so bad being one of us."

He said tomorrow would be a treat: he'd arranged for us to observe an art class in a private school on an army base, funded by the feds.

That night Peg told me on the phone that Scott had broken several dishes, helping her dry them. His hands began to shake and he couldn't grasp anything. The moment passed, but even Scott seemed worried now. "He said, 'Mom, what's happening to me?' I didn't know what to tell him," Peg said.

"He's got to see another doctor."

"I think he knows that now. But he wants to wait for you. He needs you, Jon. He's afraid to come out and say it—he doesn't want you to think he's scared."

"Poor guy." I rubbed my eyes. The motel room was all dull brown, except for bright orange pillows. On the television, a home improvement enthusiast hacked through a blond, varnished wall with a Skilsaw. "I'll be back Friday," I said. "In the meantime, ask your obstetrician if he knows a specialist who can help."

I heard the exhaustion in her voice, and cursed myself for this trip. She said my dad had called. He'd been falling down a lot, but otherwise he and my mother were fine.

"Our parents are old and frail," I said.

"Yes," Peg said. "And we're *young* and frail."

I promised I'd check with her every couple of hours; if Scott had another major episode I'd rush right home.

The saw guy's wall collapsed into a field. Sunlight glinted off his shocking silver blade.

Next day we stopped at a mall. Moon needed to buy his wife a gift. "It's her birthday tomorrow," he said. "If I don't bring her something I'll have incoming all next week—pots, pans, coffee cups. Woman has an *arm*."

A sign in the parking lot said, "Your Military Dollars at Work—Building a Bigger, Better America for Us All."

High school kids with spiked hair and jagged silver braces ran past the mall's central fountain, where the water was pink. My mind was locked on Scott; family laughter seemed to mock me. We passed a middle-aged man eating cotton candy, wearing a slick pompadour, a Western-style shirt, and designer boots. Someone should tell him Elvis is dead, I thought.

Banks of televisions blared Baghdad, *Gidget*, and *Ghostbusters* at us; shoes stacked in windows yawned like hungry mouths; near the snack shops, video arcades boomed end-of-the-world sounds.

A young mother held her daughter's hand in front of a used-appliance store. Together they stared at their own pale faces in the glass doors of revolving microwave ovens.

I realized I was crying. I stepped into a men's room to gather myself. Cold water. A moment to hide in a stall. I'd lost my bearings completely. The *whole West* was a lethal funhouse stocked with secret codes and dangerous toys. Where could my family go?

Scottie looked so solid in the picture I carried in my wallet. Handsome, peaceful, assured. What had I done to him, bringing him to this land of salt and sand and wind, this howling ghost-country?

Lynn knocked on the stall door. A short, sharp bark: "Jon. You ready to go?"

I was beginning to hate this man. Everything was a test with him. He was waiting for me to prove myself somehow.

Back on the road, past gas ranges, trailer hitches, bathtubs, sinks, the endless et cetera country folk scatter on their lots. Most of these people were in business for themselves. A kind of hope-in-despair. Every falling-down house I saw had a sign out front: "Car repair," "Cabinets made," "Stained glass," "Bunnies 4 Sale." Whole families rocked in sagging wooden swings, smoking and drinking and staring at the highway. Idle entrepreneurs.

On the outskirts of the army base a man stood on a sidewalk in front of a car lot. He flashed a hand-lettered sign at the road: "Will Work for Food." Behind him, red, yellow, and silver Hondas, hoods open, like yapping, hungry birds.

In the classroom the children slept through their art lesson, practicing the pose—heads on desks—they'd need in junior high. The school's curriculum was boredom. Were Scott and Dana this distanced from their teachers at home? I imagined the local fathers, filthy with dust or factory grease, doubled over with pulled muscles, calloused hands, yelling at all these little dreamers; in the mornings their mothers woke them so they could walk to school to sleep some more.

That night the moon was wild, licking the toothy rim of the hills.

At dinner Lynn surprised me. "Your boy," he said. "Is he all right?"

I peppered my potato. He and Moon and I were sitting in a motel coffee shop. "Yes. Why?"

He waved his hand. "Reports—you know, you hear things. Seems I've heard he's had some problems."

Careful, I thought. "He's fine."

"Good. So he's not liable to go off and do something that'll jeopardize himself or you?"

I set my knife on my plate. "What do you mean?"

"I'm just thinking of you, Jon. Your job. Your ability to concentrate." He poured Thousand Island on his salad. "Any number of things can distract a man from his work. It's easy to put the wrong foot forward."

I didn't like this: his lecturing tone. The *marching* feel of this whole damn trip. I wanted to reach across the table and hit him in the gullet with a quick left jab. "Why don't you just say what's on your mind, Lynn."

He assured me I was overreacting. My job, my happiness, my inclusion in the community—these were his only concerns. "Fitting in," he said. "Becoming one of us. That's my dearest wish for you, Jon." I believed him, though it was clear as he spoke that his motives had more to do with efficiency than compassion. I felt I had a clue now as to why he'd brought me here. His kindness was sincere, but his interest wasn't really personal. He could drop it as quickly as he'd lost the bug for acting.

Simply put, I was one of the army's decisions, a *strategy* to which Lynn had committed manpower and money (not enough); he couldn't let me fail.

"You're a good man with a good head on his shoulders. I knew that when we met. But sometimes there are problems. . . . For example, there's a radical element in town—I suppose every community has to bear a cross like this—bullheaded people who refuse to go with the status quo. They can seriously confuse a newcomer."

I watched him closely. "Who are we talking about here?"

"You know. Those women at the Test Site. Shrill damn housewives with nothing better to do. . . ."

So. He knew what Peg was up to. He knew everything about us. "What does this have to do with my son?"

He spread his hands. "Your son, your wife—I just don't want you getting distracted," he said.

"Major." I shoved my chair back a little. "What my family does—what we think, what we believe—is our business. I told you, I'm not in the army."

His lips stiffened. "You're not in some goddam movie, either, Jon." He shook his head impatiently. "I'd hoped this tour would give you a broader perspective, increase your respect for the good people at the core of this nation—maybe inspire you toward patriotic art. In more practical terms: your job depends on the military economy, on accommodating yourself to your surroundings. You're smart enough to know that. I hope your family is, too."

I had nothing more to say to the son of a bitch. I swirled spinach into rings around my plate.

"Can't you feel the rightness and rigor of all you've seen?" he said. "Comprehensive networks reaching out, designed to compensate for their own internal flaws, to form ever-expanding patterns of security and force, positioning and repositioning to meet all global shifts within a hairbreadth of acceptable margins of error—"

"What the hell are you talking about?" I said.

He stared at me.

"Cold wars come and go, but hot matériel will be with us always? Is that the story?"

"Forget it," he said. "Just forget it." He said he had business on base, and asked Moon to keep me entertained.

"Sure," said the pilot, tight with all the tension at the table. He smiled. "I know just the thing to relax you."

I told him I'd rather go to bed. He insisted on taking me out. Another test. I'd flunked one too many tonight.

Moon drove us into a small, dark town. He parked the sedan in a lot beside a sign: "El Típico Ballroom." The place looked like a pizza box hit by a truck.

Inside, battered Formica tables, unlighted candles in bottles. A wooden dance floor. Twenty or thirty soldiers—all white—moved around the room, talking, buying drinks. Moon ordered us a pitcher of ale. I was so angry at Lynn I thought my heart would burst. "Donaldson's a smart man," Moon told me. "You'd best follow his advice. In the meantime, enjoy yourself."

A few minutes later a wiry Hispanic in a red shirt and orange tie hopped onstage, followed by a single yellow spot. He announced, with not much conviction, "Gentlemen, for your pleasure, here tonight, the most whore of the world: Chi Chi María."

He stepped back and a dark-skinned teenaged girl wearing only a towel took the stage. The soldiers cheered. The MC, scowling, stuck a coin in a jukebox; a scratchy Tex-Mex tune assailed the room.

Chi Chi María wasted no time with the towel. It dropped to the stage and she wriggled a bit, no pretense at doing a dance. I thought of Peg, her smoothness, her grace. The girl ran her fingers over her tiny hips, her pubic hair, then up to her breasts. She cupped them in her palms, gazing at the wide brown nipples as though she wanted to kiss them. Her hair was thin and dark, tinged with gold in the dim yellow light. She luxuriated in the curls, rubbing them in waves across her face. Pounding cymbals; flat accordions wrapped Latin rhythms round a stout German polka.

The soldiers hooted, but a strange calm had touched them. They'd settled like children who'd just been fed. I felt it too.

"She is hot," said the wiry man. "Hot for you—all of you, all at once. She is stinking and wet, a bitch of an ass of a *puta*. She is worthless and dirty, a stinking hot piece of bitch in the street, and she laughs at you, at your mother, she breathes bad and hot in your ear and your mother cries and you cannot stop yourself, you want to beat her for being such a hot little bitch, such a bad little hot piece of bitch."

The performance was extraordinary: the more he defiled her, the more erotic she seemed. A seductive young *llorona*. Without even moving, she became the most sensual creature alive. Her boredom enraged us; each man in the room was stunned with hatred and sadness and lust. The intensity of the soldiers' stares on her body was explosive.

From the stage she leaned forward, close to me, rubbed her left breast in one hand, and with the fingers of the other spread her small vagina.

Under heavy makeup, bruises covered her cheeks and chest.

She kissed me, snarling, part of the act; instinctively I returned her kiss with fervor, even anger—vague and boundless and harsh.

When El Típico closed its doors at two, Moon was just getting started. I asked him to return me to base, but he insisted on "one more little stop." He said he was roaring now and needed his engines cooled.

"I didn't notice any civilians in the club," I said.

"That's right. Those are *our* girls. I had to explain you to the manager when we first walked in. The townies know they'll get their heads busted, they show up there."

We drove through the desert, past electronics firms and storage facilities, then out by some irrigated fields: wild onions and beets. I rolled down my window, listened to the click and *chrrr* of the sprinklers. Wonderful old mailboxes made of mower parts, milk cans, backhoe ditch diggers, wagon wheels, crankshafts, and cream separators lined the road by warped wooden signs for hairsprays and soaps.

Moon's destination was a red-light ranch. A week later, back in Tilton, Lynn would apologize to me for the man's "boorish behavior." Moon was suspended for breaching ethics, though clearly his mistake wasn't stopping at the brothel—*those* were the army's girls, too—but taking a civilian along. I wasn't meant to see it. That night, Moon was too drunk to think. He talked about the whores he'd known in Saigon, in the Papillon Bar behind the Two Moons Café. "Best fucking women in the world," he said. "This one bitch, really good English—every night she'd grab me by my prick and say, 'Little monk in his hood, kneel to pray.'" He laughed until he choked. "'Little monk stand up?'"

I thought of the bruises on Chi Chi María's skin. The car hurtled over a metal cattle guard in the dirt. Six trailer homes circled by a chain-link fence, milky with moonlight, formed a staggered hexagon in a field: the "Four-Star Love Nest." To get there we wound down a stony road; as we approached the gate,

Moon flashed his lights. I heard a loud buzz, and the gate swung open.

Red velvet, faded and stained near the floorboards, lined the front parlor's walls. A white couch curled around the room, covered with tight, slick plastic.

The madam—"I prefer the word 'manager,' " she told me—embraced Moon and gave him a sloppy kiss. Three art deco floor lamps illuminated small velvet paintings of Don Quixote and sad circus clowns above her desk.

"Girls," she called down a narrow mildewed hallway. "We've got company. Shake it back there!"

Eight young women in bright silk teddies entered the parlor, formed a snaky line before us. Beautiful but weary, rough-edged, and as bored as the stripper who'd kissed me, they pretended to be happy to see us. Only one didn't smile.

"Introduce yourselves, girls," said the manager.

"Hi, I'm—"

Cherry, Lulu, Bunny. I don't remember all their names.

One of the women resembled Linda, my high school love; I had to turn away from her. It was too sad to see those familiar features aged and ragged, and in a place like this: a long fall from innocence, a distance too far for me to travel.

Moon grabbed the one who hadn't smiled. A redhead with long, pale legs, she escorted him glumly down the hall.

"I'll just sit and wait," I said.

The manager—her name was Elk—said, "Something wrong with my girls?" Not at all, I said. She told me I'd get the standard army discount. "Any friend of Moon's is a friend of ours." No thanks, I said, I was just along for the ride, I was a happily married man, I'd prefer to wait.

"Suit yourself," said Elk. "He won't take long." She seated herself at her desk. All but one of the girls disappeared, a short blonde in boots and a bra. She sat near me and leafed through an issue of *Redbook*. The couch's plastic covering was cool and stiff.

I tried not to picture all the wretched spills there over the years.

The young woman closed her magazine and smiled at me. "Are you sure you don't want to fool around a little? Just to pass the time?" She was lovely beyond all reason. I could still taste Chi Chi María's kiss.

"Thanks, no," I said. I thought of my mother's oil field woman—the hooker who'd stolen her father.

"I see. You'd feel bad about the wife?"

"Yes."

I wondered what had caught my grandfather's eye. A coy glance, a twist of hips?

The unholy fascination of whores.

Could I be stolen? Was *I* capable of betrayal? In the abstract, yes, I thought, but that wasn't where I lived. It wasn't the weight of conscience that kept me faithful to my family. It was the weight of my children—my skin's memory of their touch, their need, and of Peg's.

But the body yearns. I imagined telling the woman beside me she was stunningly beautiful. In fact, I said, you've expanded my vision of what a woman can be. "I think if I touched you I'd be haunted, knowing I'd never see you—or anyone like you—again."

In my mind she rose and brushed my shoulder. Tears came to her eyes. "That's the nicest thing anyone's ever said to me." She kissed my cheek.

Actually, bored with her magazine, she simply vanished down the hall.

Moon took longer than Elk had predicted. Too drunk to respond. Soldiers and women. Sex as sport. What would happen to Dana if we stayed in Nevada? She'd wind up dating the high school quarterback, whose future was a hole in the ground in Chugwater, Wyoming. And that was the *best* scenario. I shivered.

Elk was sorting fifty-dollar bills. She glanced at me. "You're not a spook," she said, "or an operative."

"No. I've never been in the service. I'm an arts—I mean, I work in Tilton, Nevada."

She brightened. "Really? I grew up near there, north of Vegas."

"By the Test Site?"

"Yep. A lot of us old army brats live in these hills." She said she remembered the blasts at night—they used to frighten her as a girl. Then she laughed. She recalled the Civil Defense films she'd seen in school. "There was one called *Bert the Turtle*," she told me. "A cartoon terrapin in a hard hat and bow tie. Our class sang his little song—

> *"There was a turtle by the name of Bert*
> *And Bert the Turtle was very alert*
> *When danger threatened he never got hurt*
> *He knew just what to do:*
> *He'd duck and cover.*

"In the film," Elk said, "this goddam turtle would clam up in his shell. We were supposed to do that too in case of a Russian attack. 'You and I don't have shells like Bert, so we have to cover up in our own way'—under our desks." She chuckled.

Days later, I saw the film she was talking about. Harper and I found an old copy of it in the Tilton Public Library. In one scene, a little boy is riding his bike down a street. "Here's Tony on his way to his Cub Scout meeting," says the announcer. Then there's a flash. "Duck and cover!" Tony hops off his bike and huddles by a low brick wall near the sidewalk. Instantly a man in an overcoat and a hard hat appears.

He looked like a pervert, I thought, watching the film.

The announcer explains, "The man helping Tony is a Civil Defense worker. We must obey the Civil Defense worker. The enemy knows no mercy and has signaled his intent to conquer the world under the banner of imperialist Communism. So on school days, holidays, vacation time, we must be ready to do the right thing if the atomic bomb explodes—duck and cover!"

I thought of Scott as a child—how would he feel if his school had shown such films? Would he have made it to his teens?

"Those were crazy, crazy times," Elk said, stacking her bills. "I guess they ain't a whole lot better now, 'cept we don't hear much anymore about the Bomb."

I heard the women giggle in their rooms down the hall and thought of the laughter my mother heard in her head these days, the mocking sounds of the oil field woman who'd busted her heart. Terrors. Doubts. Warnings in the night. But my mother's curse seemed light as bread to me now, an old wives' tale, a ghost story pale in the melting glare of reality, no longer a threat to the family. We were far from the simple oil fields—and getting farther.

The night I returned to Tilton, Scott and I took a walk in the desert, out past the dinosaur track. We didn't speak at first. I waited for him to frame the discussion however he'd like.

Finally he touched my arm, and we stopped. Commercial jets warmed the air overhead; moonlight tinged fat barrel cacti in the distance, turning them to glass. They looked like giant ribbed tumblers full of creamy drinks.

"Dad. Something's happening to me," Scott said.

I nodded.

"More than my usual craziness, I mean."

"You're not crazy." I rubbed his shoulder. "Don't ever say that."

"Well. Anyway. I'm not sure what it is, but maybe I should see a doctor."

Peg had already arranged meetings with a neurologist and a psychiatrist, a week from today, but we agreed the final decision was Scott's.

"I'm glad," I said. "I think this is the right thing."

We walked a little farther, toward the hills. "Dad?"

"Yes?"

"Do you ever feel unhappy?"

"Of course, Scottie. Everyone does, now and then."

"But you keep going, right?"

"Right."

His throat tightened, and he sounded like a child. "How?"

My ribs sank into my heart. He *was* a child. That's all. "You," I said. "The people I love." My voice cracked.

"And the new baby, I suppose. Something to look forward to," he said.

"Yes."

"It's not so easy for me."

"I know, honey."

"That doesn't mean I don't love you."

"I know that too."

He looked up. "Sometimes I wish it would all just fall. You know? They get so close. Sometimes—not always—I wish the blasts . . . I just wish they'd come on ahead."

He wouldn't let me hug him, I knew. He'd reached a self-conscious age, when too much emotion embarrassed him. So we stood together, moved but goofy, stuffing our hands in our pockets.

What could I say to him? That in my darkest moments I felt the way he did? That his despair wasn't so unusual? Fearing and wishing. Anything to stop the uncertainty.

Was it comforting to learn that the not-knowing never quits?

I took his hand. "Stay with us, Scottie," I said. He could remove himself from his mother and me anytime he wanted, and I couldn't prevent him. We both knew it. The doctor was a good sign, but there were options Scottie could play. The strongest thing I could think to tell him that night was "Stay."

He seemed to listen. In the whirling, early-evening desert heat, he seemed to want to agree.

Two.

THE NIGHT BEFORE Scott's medical tests, Harper called. He wanted to meet, but not at the diner. He suggested the Moose Lodge instead.

"There's a patriot party at the Atomic tonight," he said on the phone. "Your friend the major and his pals are real pissed at what went down in D.C."

That morning the Secretary of State and the new Russian leader had signed the most comprehensive arms control agreement since the Second World War. The United States promised to scrap thousands of its multiple-warhead ballistic weapons. Also, several members of Congress had announced that day that they favored the nuclear testing moratorium bill, though the official vote was weeks away. "The news isn't all bad for our local heroes," Harper said. "While he's talking world peace, the Prez has given the go-ahead for two underground tests in the next five days. Heard any blasts lately?"

"Not for a couple of weeks."

"Well, brace yourself. They've got the green light."

Harper wanted to revisit the Dempsey site; he said he was bringing a friend who could fill in some gaps for us.

So at seven I stood on the sidewalk in front of the Moose Lodge. Thunder boomed in the beery bowling alley next door. Salt cedars rattled their branches at clear patches of sky.

Starlings picked at old M&M's wrappers in the street. The army had deemed these birds a nuisance—they nested in warm jet engines—so the researchers at Mesa Bend had developed a chemical spray to rob their wings of repellency. I'd seen hundreds of them frozen in the desert, dying, failing to fly. Grouped together now on the pavement, the birds looked like an oil slick, viscous and, under quick-blinking traffic lights, electric yellow, red, and green.

Harper pulled up in his Mercury. His sideburns had grown out and were marching now in a scruffy line toward his chin. The "Hoss" on his belt buckle gleamed like a flashlight beam.

I told him I was curious about his friend, but I wasn't keen on another visit to the site.

"It's the perfect night," Harper said. He nodded at the diner. "After the powwow breaks up over there, they'll all head down to the football stadium." The Tilton High Cougars were 8 and 0; no one doubted they'd take State. After that, a few of them—the quarterback, maybe, one or two defensive linemen, a token black—would shuttle off to the silos in Wyoming.

Harper said his friend would meet us. We pulled out of town, into shadowy, moonlit hills.

He asked if I'd learned anything on my trip. "I discovered where the army keeps its women and its booze," I said.

He laughed.

"I don't know. I'm amazed at the confidence of military men. I think anxiety's what drives most artists . . . the torment of *never quite getting it right*. But a soldier thinks even his mistakes are ordained."

"It's all in the manifest, boy—hop to!"

"Lynn—Major Donaldson—puzzles me. One minute he's a decent guy, straightforward, honest, then—"

Harper nodded. "He's one of those assholes who are always twice as loud as everyone else 'cause they're a long, long way from the top."

He turned off the highway. Dust devils stirred the site; lizards skittered over rocks. A tall man in scuffed cowboy boots and a Levi jacket waited by the road. His face in Harper's headlights was massive, square, and brown.

He didn't have a car.

We got out of the Mercury. "This here's Leonard Banks," Harper told me. I shook the man's calloused hand. "An old army buddy, and a classmate of mine at Texas Tech. He runs a small paper now down in Chinle, Arizona, but his family used to live here, where you saw the sign. I gave him a call last week, told him what you'd said. He drove up to see for himself." Harper pulled a coffee thermos out of his backseat and offered us each a cup. "We weren't in the same unit," he said. "But we humped the same swamps in Cu Chi."

"American dumping ground," Leonard mumbled.

"I told Jon this used to be Paiute land, but I didn't give him all the details. Why don't you fill him in?" Harper said.

We moved inside a circle of greasewood bushes, out of the breeze. Leonard blew on his coffee, looked me over. Clearly, he couldn't decide about me, but Harper kept nodding. Finally, Leonard told me his folks were among the many Paiutes chased off this spot in 1968 when the DOE found uranium here. He lighted a Camel, offered me one. I shook my head.

"At first the feds didn't tell us about the discovery—they claimed there were grazing problems with our goats, that the animals had overeaten and upset the ecosystem here," he said. "The men from the Bureau of Indian Affairs explained that we had to move north—for our own good, for the good of our goats. But we learned the truth and started organizing resistance. That's when the FBI got involved, and finally the fuckin' army. They said we were Communists, enemies of the state." He laughed. "They thought we were Ho Chi Minh, man. That's what they wanted. Vietnam and John Wayne. Some of these vets, I'm telling you— I *know*—now that they were back home, they were sentimental for spilled blood. The dark man's blood. We tried our best to avoid a fight."

A horned owl moaned from a prickly pear below us, in a black ravine. Leonard reached for more coffee. "Our tribal lawyers hauled the BIA into court. Said the government couldn't drill here until an environmental impact statement had been issued. That's the white man's own rules. The damn court came back and said, 'This isn't public land. It's an Indian reservation. There's no need for an impact statement.'"

He spat in the sand. "They moved in then, like a bunch of town marshals, all dressed up in their flak jackets and helmets, riding their APCs and emptying their automatic weapons. Testing the latest equipment they hoped to ship to 'Nam. It was a slaughter."

I nodded. "Harper told me."

"The ones who survived were bused into cities—Tucson, Denver, Minneapolis, where most of them went on welfare and whiskey. They weren't equipped for the cities, man. *This* was their home."

He stood and tossed a rock at a thick clump of rabbit brush. "My dad got lucky, found work in a paper box factory. But he's a rare success story."

Harper brushed dirt off his jeans. "It gets worse, Jon. East of us here—right over there—that's where 'Operation Ugly Child' took place. Ever hear of it? The navy's attempt to secretly clean up over eleven thousand live bombs, two thousand duds, and God knows how many tons of shrapnel, all dumped on public land where the military wasn't supposed to be. Couple of Las Vegas TV reporters got wind of what they were doing and blew the whistle. This was back in the seventies."

"So the DOE, trying to cover its ass, comes up with a plan they call Complex 21," Leonard said. "They claim they can clean all the waste in the West in under thirty years. Hell, they don't even know what to *do* with the waste. And we're talking billions of dollars here. Makes the S&L scandal look like a piggy-bank heist. But the locals bought it. Since then there've been no complaints."

Harper slapped my back. "So you stumbled onto some real hot property here, Jon. None of us knew there was still activity in this area."

After Harper called him, Leonard said, he drove up to talk to his friends who still lived on the old reservation.

"I thought the place had been evacuated," I said.

"It was. But in spite of all the drilling, a few of our folks keep returning, because it's sacred land to them. The army'll find them and run them off. They'll filter back in. This has been going on for over twenty years."

He said his friends mentioned the same blasts I'd heard, and strange new noises in the hills. Some of them said the land had lost all its color. "They told me, 'The world is turning gray.'"

"What does that mean?" Harper said.

"I don't know. But most of them have seen the Big Man."

I shivered. The sand was cold, even through my shoes. "The what?"

"Our fathers described the Big Man to us when we were all just kids," Leonard said. "He's huge, covered with hair. In times of distress he appears on the fringes of the plains, to warn us and prepare us for the troubles to come." I couldn't read his face, but Harper's expression told me his friend wasn't joking. He wasn't playing Indian or screwing around with the white guy. His story was on the level. "Some say he's the husband of the earth, an embodiment of natural wisdom. No one really knows," Leonard said. "But over two hundred people saw him in '68, before the army came through. And there've been over forty sightings of him this year, since the explosions began."

All the feeling had drained from my hands. "My son," I said. "He's been dreaming . . . I mean, there's this furry creature he says—"

Leonard nodded gravely. "The danger is with us. Here. Now."

"Hold on," I said. "I can't believe—"

But he and Harper had already jumped over stones, into the

shallow copper draw. They didn't know what they were looking for, but had determined to find whatever was here. I followed.

Sand churned in my face as I walked. Pastels, chalky rocks, and vibrant flowers—the ideal desert, the desert I saw in my mind—clashed with the blasted terrain I saw before me. The pleasure of cool breezes, moonlight, and dew mixed with the knowledge of evil, the stories of rape and mutilation Harper had told me.

In the desert the eye is drawn to what most clearly isn't there. Water, shelter, trees. But I couldn't look at this *nothing* without knowing, deep in my body, waste and disease—invisible components of the new West, my country's plans. My nation's possible future.

Harper knelt to examine an ashy substance in a small crater. "Engine burn," he said, rubbing the stuff in his fingers. A few yards north, we saw a bombed truck's rusty chassis. An old eagle's nest hung in the frame. Stubbly sage was making a bold comeback in a burned patch of limestone and gravel.

I scanned the still, ruined plain ahead of us. Gouged pits, twisted trees, flattened jeeps—the United States' war on Nevada.

The destruction was much worse than I'd imagined. "These tests are awfully real," I said. Each melted chunk of metal merged in my head with TV pictures of napalmed Vietnamese, scorched Iraqis (in the rare footage the world was allowed to see), mountains of corpses torched like piles of oily rags, spitting balls of their own thick fat.

"It's probably not safe to walk here unprotected," I said.

Leonard frowned at me. "The world is turning gray," he muttered. "I don't get it." As he pulled himself up on a boulder we heard the first chopper. It came from the east.

Its rotors rattled my teeth. A sudden hot wind whipped our shirts.

"Over there!" Harper shouted. We ran for a slight dune and buried our backs against it, close to the ground. The helicopter swept a spotlight over the killed targets, the craters and pits. It hovered, hawklike. A second chopper hurled a wall of sand at our legs. Its spotlight just missed us. I didn't look up. The choppers moved higher and away. We ran for the road. They swiveled back again, joined by a third, their light beams like strands of a web. The whirling air seemed to strip my skin.

We sprinted, ducked, and rolled. Finally the black machines vanished over the western hills; we were caught in only moonlight.

We lay choking on grit. "You think they saw us?" Leonard coughed.

Harper shook his head no. When we got our breath we climbed the incline toward the road. "Oh shit," Harper whispered.

I pulled up beside him. "What is it?"

He pointed to his Mercury, parked on the flat, pebbly shoulder. "I'm sure they spotted my clunker." He slapped his forehead. "It'll be a snap for them to trace the owner. Jesus."

A blast howled, several miles away.

We jumped in Harper's car and moved quietly down the highway without any lights.

At the Pit Bull Tavern, forty miles south of Tilton, where we stopped to cool off, Leonard said, "Lay low. Maybe they didn't notice the car. Wait and see what the next week brings. Meantime, I'll check into a motel, see what else I can learn from my friends."

Harper ordered a second beer. Scotch chaser. "Threw away my job," he said. "Probably wind up in jail. *First* rule of reporting: stay friendly with the powers that be, otherwise you'll never get leaks. Fuck me."

Through a cracked window I saw a rusty warehouse down the road, pale and cold under sodium lights. Its metal door swung open and shut. Its tarnished silver color made me lonely, somehow. Inside the tavern, hard-core drunks swayed to the jukebox's crooning or batted pool balls around. A moose head leered at us from a splintery pine shelf behind the bar. The moose wore a cap that said, "Harder. Faster." The bartender French-kissed the waitress.

Leonard grabbed my hand. "You're a good man," he said. "Take care of my friend Harper." Then he slipped out the door.

THE FOLLOWING MORNING, in the middle of a dust storm, Peg and the kids and I drove to the hospital. The psychiatrist wanted to speak to us all as a "family unit" before the brain man ran any tests on Scott.

Peg was tense. I was exhausted and worried from last night.

At first our brave boy was calm, but once we reached the right floor and stepped off the elevator, he claimed we'd betrayed him. "They're just going to fuck me up again!" he shouted. "You *know* what doctors do!"

He hit Barnes, the neurologist, only once. Me he pummeled several times. "Screw you, Dad! Goddammit, you just want to get rid of me!" he yelled. By now we were standing in the psychiatrist's office. A tumbleweed slammed the window screen.

"I want to help you, son." His fists swarmed my face. I slapped them away. "This was your decision, remember?"

"That's not true, that's not true—"

I grabbed him from behind and forced him into a chair. Peg cried. Dana stood in the corner. She'd been excited this morning to get away from school, but now she wanted to bolt.

The violence passed, as it always did; the psychiatrist, Robert Wren, a gentle man with a bristly gray beard, was able to seat us all quietly and begin his session. He offered Scott a cup of water.

A potted African violet filled the room's little window. On

the bookshelf, *The Freud-Jung Letters* sat next to Rilke's collected poems ("You must change your life").

Wren started with Dana. He asked her if she'd like to discuss the family. She said no. Still upset from Scottie's outburst, she glanced at Peg, then me. I nodded. "Go ahead, honey."

"Well." She avoided my eyes. "A month ago I got my ears pierced and Daddy never even noticed," she said. She squirmed and looked at her shoes.

I turned to Peg. She reached over and brushed back Dana's hair. A ruby earring flashed in the dim fluorescent light. Then I saw she was wearing lipstick—a thin red line—and her cheeks were pinker than usual. She looked so womanly. When had this change taken place? How had I missed it?

The doctor talked to her then about her needs, how they were met (or weren't), how she communicated them to us. She said it was important to her to look good, like Madonna or Cindy Crawford.

Who the hell is Cindy Crawford? I wondered. I considered my limits as a parent.

If Dana wanted to be an artist or a scholar when she grew up, I'd be right in her corner, full of golden advice. But what if she decided to be a fashion model—"like Cindy Crawford," she explained. Not only was I dumb about that world, I hated its greed and glitter. Would I be able to encourage her properly? Could I let go and give her the independence she needed?

What if she *wanted* to be the wife of a missileer?

I remembered an afternoon when she was six. She sat on the living-room floor crashing plastic cars into one another. I told her the noise made Daddy unhappy. She looked at me. "Daddy, don't you know something?" she said.

"What's that, sweetie?"

"Sometimes kids don't care if their daddies are unhappy."

I couldn't miss a trick with my baby girl. I'd already botched things with Scott.

He was reluctant to speak at first. Peg asked him to describe his dream. I hadn't mentioned Leonard's Big Man to her; I didn't know what to think of it.

Wren listened closely and said the dream was interesting. He didn't elaborate. "I'll want to speak to you later, alone," he told Scott. "But I think that's enough for now."

Barnes was ready with his tests. Peg planned to drop Dana at school while I waited with Scott, but before we left the office she pulled a tattered spiral notebook from her bag. She told Wren she'd kept a journal when Scott was born—a record of her feelings at the time. She thought it might be useful to him somehow. When he learned I'd never seen it, he asked Peg, "Would you mind if your husband had a look?"

She hesitated. This wasn't what she'd expected. "Well. No, I guess not. It's very private, though. . . ."

Wren nodded. "Share it with him. Communication is key. We'll all speak later." He disappeared down the hall.

Peg handed me the purple notebook. "Are you sure?" I said. "If it'll help."

She had an appointment with Potts later in the day. I patted her Jess-heavy belly. "Everything all right?"

"A little indigestion, from the pressure of the baby. Not too bad."

"I love you."

She smiled. "Just remember, that notebook was a long time ago, Jon. A lot has changed since then. Including me."

Barnes's first tests with Scott were designed to measure mind-to-eye coordination. "Preliminaries," he told me. "So I get a feel for the boy." He showed Scott a series of Ishihara Plates, in which subtly shaded numerals could be found—or not, depending on Scott's perception range—emerging from a thickly textured background.

"Are you having any trouble identifying shapes or forms?" Barnes asked Scott as they ran through the various procedures. "Are your edges fuzzy?"

"No. I get these real bright afterimages when you show me vivid orange."

"Any shading in the image?"

Scottie shut his eyes. "Just white."

"All right, all right, fine."

Barnes assured me they'd be at this for a while. I gave my little buddy a smile, then went to sit in the waiting room. Three middle-aged women and one old man leafed through *People* magazines. I opened Peg's purple notebook. The cover was about to fall off the rings, the paper was thin and yellow. Fourteen years ago. Scottie's debut. The dust of another life.

I turned to the first page and read:

> Scottie.
>
> My first and second child.
>
> Your mother's always wanted to be a writer, hon, a poet, but these days I give myself to dance, and all I do is scribble my thoughts in a notebook. I save whatever I can. I hope these hasty words along with the pictures and tape recordings we'll make of you growing up will preserve for you a little of the world you graced with your arrival.
>
> My first and only child: little visitor from deep within my bones. I call you my second child too because you're not the first to be conceived. Many years ago before I knew your father . . . I wasn't ready, I wasn't in love, and I put a stop to it all.

I didn't know if I should go on. Reading these words seemed a terrible violation of Peg's privacy. The intimacy, the sudden presence of the past, were bound to be bittersweet at best.

> When I was a girl, a few years older than you'll be in another few years, my girlfriends and I used to sneak into a grass field behind my mother's house in Texas. We played this little game— we'd steal our mother's sewing pins and stick them into apples.

One of my friends was Irish and she swore, according to old Irish lore, if you stuck nine pins into a fresh apple and threw the tenth pin away, you'd dream of your future husband that night. You had to tuck the apple under your pillow for the trick to work.

I remember once beneath the sheets rolling an apple up and down my thighs (they were just sprouting soft black hairs), cradling it, cool and smooth except for the stem, between my legs. . . .

My girlfriends got misty, smudged sorts of looks in their eyes, talking of men.

Once I asked your father if boys ever dreamed of gleaming wives. He laughed. "My friends and I used to sneak behind my house with full-color pinups of Ursula Andress," he said. "That's about as far as our imaginations went."

He's a good man, your father—raised in Texas too. Sometimes I wish he were a bit more aggressive—bolder—in his approach to the world. But he's solid. Decent.

Peg's familiar, crabbed handwriting was a comfort. The people in her story pained me already, though: almost forgotten, they were virtually strangers, though images were starting to jell in my mind. The clothes they wore (Peg's old bell-bottomed jeans), their hairstyles, their attitudes and experiences—silly old reruns late at night.

Bolder? More aggressive?

Years ago, when I first met Peg in Santa Fe, she was touring with a women's ballet troupe. I was studying New Mexico's arts budget. She was the most physically expressive woman I'd ever encountered. We laughed at the coincidence that we both lived in Houston. A month later, when we'd each returned to Texas, I phoned her for dinner. She was dating someone, a banker, *my* banker as it happened, but she didn't drop me from her life. We felt an attraction, a grab, at the very least a tug—the emotional equivalent of a stubbed toe, perhaps. We had a series of coincidental half-meetings in restaurants and galleries, hurried conversations, and one night, when we both failed to float safe excuses, a half-attempt at sex. Peg stopped us. She was still partially committed to the banker, she said, and could only go so far.

I began to phone her every day. I suggested we meet in disaster areas (earthquakes, tornadoes) where buildings and electrical power had been halved. We could sit together in candlelight, I said, sipping straight Half-and-Half (leaving it unfinished, of course) and listen to bootleg tapes I'd bought in college. I had the Beatles in rehearsal: they ran through parts of songs, then quit. "I'll only wear half my clothes if you'll just wear half of yours," I said. In time, she dumped the banker (I closed my account with him) and moved in with me.

I had no romantic illusions about Peg. I was never intrigued by the mystery of unattainability. I simply felt lucky and at home when I heard her voice.

She was restless, though, at first. Our joint therapist described her condition as "low-level depression." He said she was suffering from poor self-esteem, stemming from her childhood (her father was a stern Lutheran minister). "Until she corrects her self-image," the doctor told us, "she can't be happy." This may have been the case, but it seemed to me at the time that Peg's biggest problem was low-level horniness: a constant mild ache, wherever she was, to run her hands along the naked flesh of a stranger.

I was fairly well acquainted with this sort of thing myself. But I felt a person had to be disciplined, otherwise you left sticky messes in your wake.

Peg's always been obsessed by the power of the body. Sometimes, even now, her sheer physicality, both in and out of bed, surprises me—inscrutable, like the seductive strength of the "Love Nest" ladies or the woman in the oil field—but never more so than when she was giving birth to our children.

I returned to the notebook:

I worry I won't be able to give you what you need, Scottie. My own mother didn't have enough love to go around. Somehow my sister, Pat, and I sensed this, even as kids. Mom had had two miscarriages before we were born—both girls. To this day she keeps the booties and blouses—small enough to fold inside a shoe box— she bought for our dead older sisters. I used to dress my dolls in these mysterious, brightly colored shrouds.

I'm telling you all this because, for better or worse, it's bound to have had some effect on my own approach to motherhood.

Anyway, by the time Pat and I arrived, Mother, I think, had used up her heart. Expectations and disappointments had wrung her out, like a rag. She used to say she was a genius at outliving and burying the people she loved: her parents, her own sister, two of her children.

As if her other two children and her husband had never shared her house.

Each week she'd take me to visit my sisters' graves. In my mind I see her kneeling over the tiny mounds of grass as though her babies were garden plants. Her heavy breasts ballooned her cotton dress like full sacks of peat ready to fertilize her carefully pruned and still-living losses.

In her head she heard them calling her. I knew from the faraway face she wore.

I used to rhyme and sing to my ghost-sisters, worry about jolting them underground, shaking dirt into their throats whenever I skipped rope or hopscotched. They were easier to care for, since I could make them up, than Pat was. In fighting for our mother's approval we bruised each other's arms, tore each other's favorite skirts (mine was yellow, cotton—I can still see the rip, like a knife wound, along the zipper, and Pat's mean little smile). With Pat my greatest joy was pinching her until she cried, then watching the red marks appear on her arm like Instamatic photos before my eyes. This terrible capacity to hate a person I loved made me wonder about being a mother. I'm not sure, even now, if I've done the right thing in serving you up like a gourmet dish to the world's awful appetite, Scott. You may as well know that. But I promise to try to do better than my own mother did—the optimism of each *new generation. The only bruises I'll ever leave in life I've already left on my sister's skin.*

It's true, I thought: at first Peg was a fearful mother—frightened of *herself*—always expecting disaster. The slightest nick on Scottie's arm sent her spinning, a frenzy the baby enjoyed. He laughed at her expressions of concern as though they were clown faces she made to amuse him. In time, his delight taught us both how to relax and give him what he needed.

Was that a skill we'd forgotten?

I remember the night he arrived, I panicked, wondering if Peg and I were stable enough to be good parents together. I'd waited all evening in the hospital with two other expectant dads who'd obviously been through the process before. They seemed relaxed, and were having a mild argument about the causes of infant-death syndrome.

I found Peg's doctor and asked him what I'd miss if I left for twenty minutes. "Go get yourself some dinner," he said. "She'll be all right."

I hopped into my Honda and raced without thinking through town. Yellow lights burned in windows up and down the neighborhoods. Dinnertime. Squash, potatoes, beets. I felt keenly the rhythms of the families around me.

Video stores lined the highway. Life-size cardboard Rambos stood in the store windows, preening. Slick muscles and guns. Several filling stations appeared to be failing along that strip of road. Owners had taped hand-lettered signs to their pumps: "Sorry, No Gas."

In a gravel parking lot just outside the city, teenage boys crumpled cans of beer. They carried bowling balls in rhinestone-studded bags.

I imagined my son sitting beside me in the car, his umbilical cord wrapped like a seat belt around his waist. Take a look around, kid, this is it, I thought.

Past fields of mint and wild onion I drove. Their loamy smells stung tears into my eyes. For a long time, with the radio on, I didn't slow down or stop.

Peg had taught me a prayer to pass on to the child:

"Angel of God—come on, Jon, do it with me," she'd said.

"My guardian dear," I recited.

"To whom God's love."

"Entrusts me here."

"Ever this day . . . Jon, *ever this day* . . ."

"I forget."

"Be . . ."

"At my side."

"To light, to guard."

"To rule and guide."

I whispered that prayer to myself every night now for my son.

At noon, during a break from the doctor's wearying tests, I sat with Scott in the hospital lunchroom. Our food was gritty with sand. "How do you feel?" I said.

"I'm scared, Dad."

"I know." I patted his wrist. "Your mother and I will make sure nothing terrible happens. I promise."

He nodded. "Is that Mom's notebook?" he said.

"Yeah." I'd laid it on the table next to my tray.

"What's in it?" he asked.

"The usual stuff. You know. What a great kid you were."

"Were. Right."

"Still are, still are." I ruffled his hair.

After lunch there were X-rays, needles, coiled wires. A young technician plugged the wires into banks of machines. They looked like sound boards at a rock concert.

Wildly waving steel arms spat jets of purple ink onto yellow graph paper.

Magnetic resonance imaging: Scott's brain—actually, his whole body, strapped inside a plastic tube the width of an outdoor garbage can—was placed inside a magnetic field so a computer could find the hydrogen atoms in his head and turn them into pretty pictures.

While most of this was going on, I returned to the waiting room and Peg's tiny writing. Since she'd kept her journal hidden, I expected to find in it troubling revelations, admissions of unhappiness, her restlessness, maybe even details of affairs she'd had, or thought about, our first year together. None of that was here. Still, the milder shock of uncovering her daily worries was somehow disturbing: a clear reminder that, no matter how well you learn someone, she's still out of reach.

I smoothed a page:

> *Last night I lay in bed with you and your dad. I couldn't stop my fears about the world. You're so helpless and small. Jon rubbed baby oil on my belly, to calm me. You whimpered something but didn't wake. It sounded like "Mommycome" though of course it couldn't have been.*
>
> *Soft sleep, Scott. Easy dreams. I'm already here.*

I closed the notebook and pictured Peg in her hospital bed after giving birth to Scott. Sometimes when you've been joking with a friend, then you shake hands and part, you may still have the trace of a smile on your lips—a little facial echo of a happy moment. That's how she looked.

She reached out her hand to me. The space around her pillow smelled of roses (I'd bought a dozen at an all-night Safeway when I'd driven back to town) and rubbing alcohol.

It's the biggest regret of my life, now, that I wasn't with her when Scottie was born. I should've been there with ice or water or a tape of her favorite music to help her relax.

That night in her hospital room neither of us mentioned our fears about our marriage. We both understood that, for better or worse, Scottie had changed things forever.

"Hi," I said. I kissed her eyebrows.

"Have you seen him?"

"I've seen him."

"Does he have all his fingers and toes?"

"Yes, and he came with his own little American Express card."

Peg smiled. "Jon," she said.

"I love you," I said.

"I think I want to rest for a minute."

"Okay," I whispered. "Angel of God . . ."

She squeezed my hand. "My guardian dear . . ." But she slept before I reached the next line.

Jon closes his eyes and finds his way inside. I grip him hard and try to brake his pace with my hips. He senses my pressure, slows. I hear apples fall outside our window. They thump, then roll in short half-circles over moist pads of grass. One apple, two . . . now Jon, who's a kind, attentive lover when he's relaxed, feels me drifting, pulls me back with his tongue. His elbows clap my sides like fruit pounding ground. I imagine the dark, bruised skins of the Golden Delicious. . . .

Later I wake in the thick, cool black of our room. My neck straddles Jon's arm. His wrist muscles spasm; my head has put his arm to sleep. I roll over. I hold his numb hand. We suffer each other sweetly for the briefest, and deepest, of pleasures.

I felt my face turn red. I glanced to see if others in the waiting room had lowered their magazines to stare at me.

Bless her heart. Bless her lovely body and her mind.

This thought reminded me of the books on Wren's office shelf, and a passage of Freud's I'd read in college about the power of women's bodies. As I recall, he said men are afraid of women because they appear to be castrated.

Jesus. My head was in a whirl. I rubbed my eyes.

Around midafternoon Barnes interrupted my reading to show me an MRI shot of Scottie's skull. His brain looked like an egg yolk in a spoon. "Nothing abnormal," Barnes said. "Thought you'd like to see. Couple more tests here, and we'll be through for the day."

I stretched, walked down a hall to a vending machine, traded two good quarters for a cup of miserable coffee, then returned to my long-ago wife:

Stop pushing.
Stop pushing.
Stop pushing.
What? I say. Stop pushing? But it's my life. I'd have pushed the rest of my days to get Scottie born. In labor, my whole existence was locked inside that rhythm. I dream about it still.
Stop pushing, voices tell me, he's here.
I wake in the night and it's true: here he is, thick as a pillow. I remember pushing—how long?—but I don't recall the pain. When I came to myself in the hospital I discovered gauze and white patches on my arms. I looked pieced-together, like a radio. "You bruised yourself a little, thrashing around in OR," the doctor told me.
"Isn't it a pain in the ass," friends ask me, "when he screams and cries and you have to pace the house with him all night?"
Yes yes, of course, but it's like being in love, I tell them. You don't mind it when your lover turns to you in the night.
Keep pushing, keep pushing, he's here.

The rest of the pages were blank.

I closed the cover, felt its soft, worn texture—the aged skin Peg feared she had now, but didn't.

The afternoon seemed to slow; the light held still and all the motion out the window—trucks, birds, sidewalk strollers—grew slack.

I'd felt this same slowing-down in a minor car wreck I'd been in once. A drunk college buddy of mine rammed us into a tree. I remember watching the oak loom larger as we approached it and knowing we were going to hit it; I remember wondering if I'd be hurt and who would miss me if I died—yet the skid and the impact couldn't have lasted more than three seconds. Something happens to people's senses in a moment of danger or high awareness. Time's out.

As I explained to Wren when we met again to discuss my reaction to the journal, Peg's words had a similar effect on me that afternoon in the waiting room. My own memories overlaid hers, like fresh brushstrokes on a canvas. I cried for those people and their happy baby boy. Good folks coping the best they could, with only a small, blurry picture of the future.

Too late to warn them now of the dangers that lay ahead.

And maybe, after all, they'd turn out okay.

That night, I drew the plastic partition that separated the kids' beds from ours. Peg smiled and yawned and drifted. I smoothed my hand across her face. Despite all our moves, our troubles with Scott, the normal wear and tear of marriage, she'd grown easily into herself over the years. Working, relaxing, making love, she fit her body so well, filled her space with casual grace: a dancer's trick, I supposed—lovelier than anyone I'd ever seen, even the young beauty in the "Four-Star Love Nest."

I stroked her thighs, her rippling dancer's muscles. "Scottie held up really well today," I said. "I was proud of him."

"Two *weeks* to process their tests?"

"They have to send them to Vegas. Patience, patience." I gathered her breasts in my hands. To hell with Freud. "Would you like me to be bolder?" I said. "More aggressive?"

She blushed. "You read my journal."

"Twice."

"Oh God. Well?"

"A model couple," I said. I unzipped her skirt. "The husband loved his wife."

"Yes."

"And she put up with him."

Peg pulled me under the sheet. "Oh, more than that. She adored him."

"Even though he shrank from the world?"

"That was years ago."

"No complaints now?"

"Only that I don't get enough of you."

"You're a much better mother than your mom was."

"Thank you." She smiled, rolled over, and said it was my turn.

"For what?" I said.

"An embarrassing confession. Come on."

"All right," I said. "I cried when John Lennon died. And when Ringo turned fifty."

"Softie."

"I wish you'd start a new journal. I want to hear the rest of the story."

GO TO BED.

I don't want to go to bed.

Then I'll tell the paddle to smack your bottom. Paddle, smack the bottom of this bad little girl who won't go to bed.

I don't want to smack the bottom of the bad little girl.

(Dana laughing.)

Then I'll tell the match to scorch you into splinters. Match, ignite this nasty paddle which won't smack the bottom of the bad little girl who doesn't want to go to bed.

Not me. I don't have any interest in scorching the paddle into splinters.

Then I'll tell the bucket of water to snuff you out. Hey, bucket of water, slosh on over here and snuff out this silly match that doesn't have any interest in scorching this nasty paddle (a *most* disagreeable paddle, unshaven and rude) which refuses to smack the bottom of the bad little girl who insists she won't go to bed.

But I see no reason to snuff out this match.

Then I'll tell the mouse to slurp you up. Mouse, slurp up this water which sees no reason to snuff out that match (that match growing dumber by the minute) which has no interest in scorching the face of the paddle that won't smack the bottom of this bad little girl who hates going to bed.

No thanks. Not thirsty.

Then I'll tell the cat to eat you. Cat, will you kindly eat this mouse who won't slurp up the water which refuses to snuff this match that has no desire to scorch the odious paddle which still hasn't smacked the bottom of this bad little girl who should've been in bed an hour ago?

Yes, I'll gladly eat the mouse, said the cat.

Said the mouse, Then I'll slurp up the water in the bucket.

Said the water in the bucket, I'll snuff out the match.

Said the match, All right I'll scorch the paddle into splinters.

Said the paddle, Show me the bottom of the bad little girl.

Giggling, Dana said, "Okay, I'm going to bed now."

"Good night."

"Good night. Daddy?"

"Yes?"

"Will there be loud noises in the sky again?"

"I don't know, honey."

"Sometimes I sleep right through them."

"Yes, you're a brave little girl. Nothing's going to hurt you."

"I *am* brave, aren't I?"

"Very brave."

"Okay. Good night."

"Good night."

"Daddy?"

"Yes, Dana?"

"How brave?"

"Very brave."

"I love you."

"Love you too."

Tonight I'm sweating under buzzing lights, listening to the mothers plan a bake sale. The room's stone walls, painted green, are plastered with framed crayon portraits of George Washington and bald eagles who *look* like George Washington.

This is the Steering Committee of Dana's school—what was called, when I was a kid, the PTA. I'm the only man here. Most of these women are army wives. Our committee work twice a month gives them the only chance they have to make their own decisions. The small tasks they tackle with relish, but when something major comes along (complaints about a textbook or a teacher), they defer to me. A timid liberation from tradition.

I volunteer to make banana bread for the bake sale. It's hard for me to concentrate tonight. On Tuesday my Rauschenberg plan fell through, so I hastily mounted a show entitled "Fifty Years of Comic Books"—original Spiderman, Batman, and Hulk covers along with artists' sketches. The exhibit had toured California for months; it was easy to lure this way. I'd thought of including Warhol and Lichtenstein, to demonstrate pop art's affinities with funny books, but finally I'd opted for simplicity. The opening was a hit. Still, ticket sales totaled only a third of our operating costs. I spent the day reckoning losses.

While the mothers make pie assignments I step into the next room to check on all our kids. They're shaping, in clay, the monstrous heads of their parents and teachers. The room is hot; the children have removed their shoes and lined them up by the wall.

The boys are belligerent and loud. They like to throw things. The girls sit patiently, whispering to each other.

I stand in the doorway watching the kids, keeping an ear on the mothers, my colleagues, these wonderful ladies struggling to assert themselves. My presence here is a fight to enter *their* world, the "feminine" world of child care and nurturing.

There aren't any models for what we're trying to be. The roads our elders paved for us have all been erased, I think, by changing, less certain times.

I stare at the children's empty shoes. It's as though the kids have flown away to find and inhabit the adult bodies walking around in the world, waiting just for them.

Peg reminded me we'd promised the kids a trip to Vegas, but this was an awkward time. Despite the new show's success, the pressure was still on to redeem myself after the Beckett fiasco; besides, lately Vegas, like Los Angeles, had erupted into riots. Each day the papers printed pictures of young black men marching into town from rotting housing projects, toward the million-dollar casinos. The hotel marquees shouted, "Free Vacations!" and "Strike It Rich!" The gangs waved signs saying "Lost Vegas" and "Mississippi West—Stop Police Occupation of Our Neighborhoods." On television I watched a teenage boy hurl a stun grenade at a fluttery line of cops; in the next instant an armored personnel carrier—borrowed from the air force—chased the boy down an alley of scattered trash, broken windows, and burned-out cars.

Commercials claimed the "fun never sets in Vegas"; casino owners, interviewed, said the danger zones were far from the "beautiful heart of everyone's dream."

Meanwhile, my father had given me another reason to stay in Tilton: last week he'd fallen and broken his ankle. He told me on the phone he'd slipped in the doorway of Mom's room at the retirement home—the janitors had waxed the floor that morning. Mom said the oil field woman had pushed him. I didn't want to leave, even for a weekend, in case he called again, needing me back in Dallas.

Scott didn't mention his medical tests, though he was as impatient as Peg and I to hear the results. He went quietly to school each day, did his homework every night. His on-again, off-again ailment drained us all, like hunger or longing: there was never an end, a fixed point to anticipate.

Peg said we should do something special for Dana; she'd been heroic while we paid so much attention to Scott.

"What would you like?" I asked her one Saturday afternoon.

"I want to see your office," she said.

"That's all?"

"Yep."

"Okay, missy. You're awfully easy. Let's go." I took her downtown. She sat in all my chairs, sharpened my pencils, examined my poster collection: Nijinksy, Pavarotti, Marie Taglioni, Buster Keaton. I lavishly praised her earrings.

"Daddy, why do you like pictures and music so much?"

"Without music the world would be a mistake." I lifted her onto my desk. "A smart man named Nietzsche said that. *You* like songs, right?"

"They make me feel all fizzy inside—like a Coke when you shake it?" She reached for a poster by the window: Ingrid Bergman's kissable lips. "Daddy, is the army going to tear down your pictures?"

I asked her why she thought that. She'd heard me say Major Donaldson hated art.

"I don't know, honey. Not everybody feels the way you and I do."

She asked about my daily routines, but I sensed my job wasn't the point of this trip. Something else was bothering her. Later, as she locked the office door for me, she finally spit it out. "Dad, what will I have to do when my baby sister gets here?" she said. She squinted in the sun.

"What do you mean?"

"Will I have to tell her everything I know?"

"Only if you want to."

"Will I have to watch her eat?"

I laughed. "It won't be a pretty sight. I think maybe we can excuse you from the table."

"Will you love her more than me?"

"Not in a hundred million years, sweetie."

We walked a few blocks to Baskin-Robbins to get some chocolate–chocolate chip, and to sit in the plastic seats. Dana swung her legs. "Is Scott going to die?" she asked matter-of-factly, licking her cone. Her tongue was a muddy, snowy slope. "Is that why you're having another baby?"

My fingers tingled. "No, honey, no. He's going to get better."

"Promise?"

"Yes." I felt as though someone had knocked the wind out of me.

"I miss him. You know, when he's not just Scott. When he jumps around and acts all scary."

"Me, too. You love him, don't you?"

"I guess." She held up her cone. "It's just that he—"

"What?"

"He takes up so much room."

I nodded. She wasn't speaking of his size.

"If he was here right now, you'd get him an ice cream, wouldn't you, Dad?"

"Sure."

"So . . . can I have another one? The one he would've had? Please? Strawberry now with chocolate syrup and bananas? And maybe some peanuts on top?" She tugged my hand.

"Only if you're buying," I said. She frowned: a little girl in lipstick. I handed her the money and watched her sweep into the store.

SINCE OUR ADVENTURE at the Dempsey site, Harper had been out of touch. He was never at his desk when I called, and the people I spoke to couldn't tell me where he was.

No word from Leonard.

I looked up Harper's address one night—the Continental Arms, the only prefab apartment house in town—and poked around over there. His car was gone. No old mail in his box.

A thick plastic statue of a colonial soldier guarded the iron-rail gate.

So far, Thompson and Lynn had been benign threats. But now? What if they'd actually done something to my friend?

Shocked by this possibility, I worried more than usual when Peg designed a "Ground Zero Cleanup Hut" inside the Test Site. With the help of her friends, including the Vietnamese woman from the 7-Eleven in town, she constructed a delicate wooden shelter near Jackass Flats. Opaque red scarves, tied to the hut's central beams, hovered in the breeze. The women splashed green paint on the roof until the place looked festive and alive, like a jumbo piñata.

Inside, a slide projector cast photos of waterfalls and rain forests onto a canvas. They provided brutal contrasts to the waste and devastation of the Flats. Susie, the big Navajo woman I'd met, had sewn colorful light cotton dresses for the group; the women moved around the hut in the freeform fashion Peg had shown them. They chanted:

> *Clear the way in a sacred manner!*
> *I come.*
> *The earth is mine.*
> *The earth is weeping, weeping.*

The building and the strange, floating figures in the desert drew the local media. Reporters were ushered inside to see the slides—the ideal planet—and recruited to collect McDonald's sacks, Coors bottles, and other trash left by soldiers who'd arranged bomb tests downwind.

Peg spoke to the cameras, urged people to write their local representatives, to bolster the test ban.

The newsmen's pictures never aired. Overnight, when none of the women were around, the "Cleanup Hut" was axed and burned.

"At least we caught *someone's* attention," Peg said the following morning, kicking through the debris.

"Be careful," I told her. "Remember Tiananmen Square?" We shielded our eyes from blowing ash. "These old men'll only be pushed so far."

"Are you wimping out on me?" she said.

"No." I cradled her growing belly. "Just watch yourself."

The rest of the day I couldn't stay focused in the office. I phoned various friends in Texas and New York, seeking cost estimates for bare-bones productions of *Speed the Plow* or the traditional *Nutcracker* for Christmas.

Harper still wasn't in.

I zipped through my Rolodex of worries and called my father. He'd fallen again, reinjured the ankle and strained his hip. Reluctantly, he'd taken a room in the retirement home—temporarily—so he could receive regular care and be near my mother. I wondered if he'd ever get out again. The musty medicine smells, the all-night moans, were enough to kill anyone's spirit, especially a frail old man's.

He sounded weak as a drizzle. "Oh Jon, listen, just in case— my will and all my legal papers are in the top drawer—"

"Dad, let's not go into that now, all right? Are you feeling better?"

"I feel like a crash derby."

"Well, what do the doctors say?"

"The medication they've got me on speeds up my heart. They don't know why. And this damned ankle—I don't heal as fast as I used to, Jon, and there's all sorts of sickness in this joint. That's why I'm telling you, all my investment information—"

Caught between my parents and my kids, I was failing, unable to meet their needs. I felt like a puppy, eager to please but too stupid to learn the standard tricks.

Dad had given up. I heard it in the low, uncertain tremble of his voice. He didn't *expect* to get out of the home. As usual, he insisted he didn't want me back in Dallas. I made him promise to call me the minute he felt worse.

Later that day Lynn stopped by my office. He carried the machete, the kukri, I'd seen in his house. "Dropping it off at the cutlery," he told me. "Get it sharpened. I hate a dull blade."

I could tell he was upset about something. His jaw was tense; the muscles inflated his face. "I know what you think," he said finally. "You think Tilton's a goddam backwater, don't you? Did it never *once* occur to you, Jon, that you might be sitting in paradise? Granted, granted, it's not postcard-gorgeous. We could use a few more lakes. So okay."

"Lynn—"

He tapped the kukri on the floor, gouging a hole in the wood. He cursed the local housewives again. "They've thrown everything off balance. By the way, Jon, I hear there may be a holdup on your security clearance—some silly snafu down the line. I'm sure we can straighten it out, but you never know. . . ."

So that was it. I rose and poured myself some coffee. "Lynn, I fully support what Peg is doing," I said. A feint to the left, a quick jab to the heart. It would be so easy. "And I don't appreciate veiled threats."

He laughed. "You still don't get it, do you?" he said. "Like your friend at the *Examiner*. You still think you're operating beyond the perimeter, away from the regular rules of engagement." He swung his kukri in the air. "This is not a fight you can win, Jon. I tell you as a friend."

He grinned, turned sharply on his heel, and left. Harper still didn't answer at the paper.

Later, walking home after work, I greeted my fellow citizens. They nodded, and pleasantly smiled.

The hut's destruction raised Peg's fervor even higher. She was determined to stage a performance that would blow the lid off Tilton once and for all. "This challenge has changed my aesthetics," she told me one night. We were making pesto and pasta for dinner.

In the past, she said, she'd believed art was a matter of craftsmanship and mastery. The modernist ideal. "But I'm beginning to see how masculine that attitude is—how tied it is to corporate thinking, manufacturing, the age of the Bomb."

I chopped basil leaves on an old dark cutting board.

"Mastery's narcissistic," she said. "Worse, it leads to exploitation—of materials, other people, the marketplace—and competition, the desire to kill your enemies. Collaboration is much more satisfying. Making it up as you go. Losing your ego. That's what these women have taught me. Maybe—I don't know—maybe that's what *motherhood* has taught me."

She stirred linguini into a pot of boiling water. "This old-fashioned image of the artist as a loner battling the odds—the hero riding off into the sunset—its time is up, Jon. Too narrow. Too selfish."

I thought of the young Jackson Pollock, isolated, independent. His dusty cowboy jacket. His dead-eye, Billy-the-Kid look. I thought of Peg's notebook: *I give myself to dance.*
I give.
As she'd always done.

On Christmas Eve, C-130 cargo planes lifted into the air, carrying food and relief supplies to the California coast where, the day before, heavy rains and mudslides had wrecked several homes. Our local newscaster called the operation a "heartwarming humanitarian gesture for the season." Behind him, brief scenes, all alike: people huddled in blankets by a soggy forest road.

Tilton marked the holiday quietly. Big Macs were half price. Lester's had a tire sale.

The TV weatherman tracked Santa on radar, offering hourly updates on his ETA. Dana got excited.

The jolly old fellow didn't stand a chance. All night we had him in our sights.

WREN PHONED. Scott's test results were ready. Peg and I gussied up, as though our finery might impress Bad News, show it our class and respectability, weaken its resolve.

Wren welcomed us into his office, poured us both coffee. He said our son's symptoms were consistent with Tourette's syndrome, a mysterious, possibly genetic disease with both physical and mental roots. "The convulsive tics, the sudden violence, the unstoppable stream of curses—Tourette's manifests itself in all these ways, also with echolalia, repeating people's words, and echopraxia, imitation," Wren said. His voice was clear and kind. "Of course, the symptoms don't always appear at once. Sometimes different combinations emerge, and the intensity changes." He said Touretters tend to test the limits of their environment, the social boundaries that box them in. "The compulsiveness, then, is a kind of straining against invisible barriers."

I rubbed my eyes. "Then Tilton is the worst possible place for him. The military presence. The rigidity."

Wren shrugged. He felt the violence could be controlled—Scott had a surplus of dopamine in the brain, he said, and this could be alleviated by the drug haloperidol—but he warned us the tics would remain.

"All his life?" Peg asked.

"Most likely."

After the Prozac disaster, Scott hated medications. I spent two days convincing him we'd kill the treatment if trouble flared.

"You promised no more," he said.

"If there's a chance this could help, Scott, I think we should try it."

"So what am I—I mean I'm—I'm going to be a freak all my life, is that it?"

"Not at all. You'll just be yourself," I said. "You'll always be the son I love with all my heart."

He hugged me and cried against my chest. "My strong, strong boy," I said. "You're the best. You're the best, pal."

He tapped my shoulder for nearly twenty minutes.

His first week on haloperidol was uneventful, though he'd had natural calm spots before. It was too early to tell if the drug was any good; I was just grateful nothing awful had happened so far.

With each passing day he seemed more aware of his own compulsions. One night he explained to me that his touching had to be symmetrical. "At first I wasn't even conscious of this," he said, "but I realize now if I tap an object—this involuntary reflex of mine?—I tap it an even number of times all over its surface. I don't know how to explain it. It's like, I have to assure myself it's really there." He pointed at a lamp across the room. "If I'm not sitting beside something, I have no desire to feel it. But if I'm near—" He reached for my face, my arms. "I need to touch."

20

WE WERE ALL WAITING for spring. Though winter was never harsh in the desert, and wildflowers grew year-round, our bodies yearned for freshness. The cycles of dormancy and renewal rolled like a fisherman's silver spinners in our blood. Warm breezes teased us late at night. We opened our windows and filled them with white porcelain pitchers ready for roses, petunias, sleek green ferns.

Tilton's mood was mixed. The House and Senate had passed the nuclear testing moratorium bill, though the President threatened to veto it. Seven top aerospace company officials were indicted for overpricing weapons parts. Locally, the army was still in charge, the town appeared to be thriving, but everyone sensed the arms industry's glory days were finished, at least for now. Tilton was waiting for a new kind of bomb to drop, a pink-slip special, zooming in under radar.

Even the international news touched us all personally that winter. Because of its mission, Tilton was part of each day's global chaos. In Ukraine, under a fog of industrial soot, previously safe wild mushrooms turned up toxic, killing several children on holiday. Iraq hid its nuclear secrets from the world. Sheep went blind in southern Chile where the ozone layer had been burned to a simple fine mist. In Eastern Europe, ethnic tribes ecstatic with pure bloody freedom slaughtered each other. Warm breezes teased us late at night. We waited and waited and waited.

One evening the Herons invited us to dinner. While the kids were getting ready, I KO'd the punching bag: a series of right crosses straight from the shoulder, each blow a strike against my periodic Tilton gloom. After Wren's diagnosis of Scott, I'd sent out a whole new batch of job applications, nationwide. Nothing. *Adjust,* I told myself. *Make the best of where you are.* But simple glimpses all around me—porch lights in the middle of the night, paint cans rusting in someone's oily old garage, pennies lost and trampled in a field—plunged me into the coldest loneliness I'd ever felt. The town seemed to speak to me of absence. Of final things.

On some nights, breezes lifted the odors of the nearby waste treatment plant my way, a smudge in the air, but gentle, forgiving somehow—all the trash that carried traces of our appetites, our private, daily affections, even as we sealed it and threw it away. I lunged at the punching bag, this child's toy that exhausted me so easily.

I remembered I'd known a boxer once. His name was Willie. He was training for the '76 Olympics in a gym next to an amateur playhouse I worked for in Dallas. At twenty-six he'd already lost most of his teeth. He sold stolen toasters out of the trunk of his Buick. He never made it to the games. Odds are, he never made it over the freeway to the finer side of town.

I lowered my head, hurled my breath, and *delivered.* One for Willie.

A fighter's choices are easy, I thought: dance, hesitate, and stay in one spot or rush right in and fuck yourself up for good.

Peg came out of the trailer. She eased herself into a lawn chair, holding her belly as if it were a gift. "You're angry," she said, watching me move. "Nervous. What about?"

I wiped my face with a dishtowel. I told her Harper had disappeared. Until I said it, I hadn't realized how much he'd been on my mind. I didn't want to worry Peg, but now I gave her a full account of what had happened that night at the Dempsey site. I mentioned Lynn's visit to my office.

She slumped.

Later, as we showered, I tried to perk us up. I soaped her shoulders. Washed her hair. "Jessie," I whispered into her navel. Peg giggled. "Jessie dear, sit still while I get that spot behind your ear."

I knelt in the tub and reeled off a series of survival tips. "You'll have an inner life, Jess. It'll intoxicate you. Cultivate it properly and you'll probably be all right in the world. I can't tell you anything more important than that.

"You'll need to know your colors. Red means danger, heat. The two aren't always the same. A steaming stew flavored with sun-dried tomatoes, a clear afternoon at the beach . . . red-hot *can* be pleasing, like a tickle."

I kissed Peg's thighs. She laughed and gasped and lost herself in the steam.

"If you were going to be a boy-child I'd tell you—half in earnest, half in jest—to pick a spot, like a dog, piss in a circle around it, and claim it as yours."

I licked her skin as I talked. She hugged herself with pleasure.

"That's all the planet is," I whispered. "Increments. A graph. One tiny square after another. But you'll be a girl."

Peg came with a shiver. Her fluids mixed on my tongue with the taste of Ivory soap.

"Pissing in a circle will be hard for you. . . ."

Beth Heron greeted us at her door wearing a "Bombs Away!" apron—a freebie from a Vegas lounge, she said. On the apron, a cartoon man held a martini to his mouth; the olive was a blimplike missile.

Zack looked like a badly raked field. His skin was gray and his hair appeared to have thinned since we'd seen him last. "Same damn flu," he muttered. "Had it the night of your play, remember? Can't seem to shake it." He poured me a beer. "I'm not contagious, though. Midge and Beth here are healthy as horses."

Scott watched him closely. The Herons eyed Scott, fearing he might break for the hills again.

On the back patio, Beth ladled barbecue sauce onto a rack of icy chickens. Flames leaped from the coals and singed her wrists. She jumped back, spilling a tray of onions. "Need a hand?" I said.

Midge interrupted us. She pushed a bowl of burbling green slush at my face. "Have some dip," she said. "Made it myself. Cheese, jalapeños, avocados."

"Is this your Aurora Fuel, Mom? I've been dying to try it," Beth said. I helped her with the onions.

"Yeah." Midge waved away smoke. "Zack's buddies down at the plant are wild for this stuff."

"Aurora Fuel?" I asked.

Midge laughed. "That's what they call it. Gasses 'em all up after lunch."

The chicken never really got done. Seated quietly around the table, we picked at it, ate what we could. Zack beamed when Peg asked him how things were going. He said he'd been promoted. "Top-secret stuff," he whispered melodramatically, widening his eyes. "James Bond, eat your heart out." He chuckled. "Actually, it's components for this new-fangled thing—I can't really talk about it." He shoveled a forkful of corn into his mouth.

I swallowed a piece of gristle. Midge's dip settled and sighed in its bowl. I took a shot. "So how *is* the Aurora?" I asked.

Zack was startled. Bingo, I thought.

"What do you mean?" he said.

"The plane. The one you're working on. How do the prototypes look? Or are you beyond that stage now?"

"How did you—?"

Midge blushed.

"Oh, it's common knowledge," I said.

"It is?"

"Sure. There aren't many secrets in Tilton." I tried to remember Harper's guesswork. "Rocket-ramjet engines, right? Four thousand miles per hour?"

Peg stared at me, shocked.

The gristle had lodged in my chest. I drained my cup of water.

Zack tapped the table with his knife. "Jon. I have no idea what you think you know, but I really can't talk about it. I'm under strict orders." He stabbed at the meat on his plate.

"It's responsible for these blasts in the sky, isn't it? Is it nuclear-powered?"

"Please, Jon. I can't say anything. I'm sorry I brought it up in the first place. Me and my big mouth." He laughed and tried to pass my comments off as nothing.

"Zack," I said. "What does it mean when the world turns gray?"

He lunged across the table. I thought he'd go for my throat, but instead he snatched my plastic tumbler and filled it again from the tap. He lowered his voice. "I'm gonna tell you something, Jon. I'm just a guy doing his job. That's all," he said. "It's not the greatest job in the world, but I'm lucky to have it." He hovered over me. His hand shook, spilling the water. "Look at California—you know how many layoffs they've had in the last eight months? McDonnell Douglas just moved most of its MD-80 production to Salt Lake City, and that's just the beginning. So I follow my orders. Gladly. Gladly, Jon." He wiped his mouth with the back of his sleeve. "I ask only enough questions to get through the day. And you should too." He handed me the cup and laid his big hand on my shoulder. "That's the way it is in this town. Got it?"

I apologized. He nodded. "Just be careful, okay?" he said.

After dinner he invited me out on his porch to share some whiskey. He smoked a cigar. The sky was bright with a crooked moon.

"My father was a cattleman," Zack said, groaning, stretching his arms. "Owned several hundred acres over in eastern New Mexico." He sat in a wicker chair. "I always hoped to work the ranch like my older brothers, but Dad didn't want me to. He said,

'Someone in this family is going to go away, get a good education, strike it rich, and do us all proud.' I was the one he'd picked." Zack laughed. "I was never so hot in school, but Dad pushed me. I was the youngest kid, his last chance."

He waved his cigar. In the moonlight, the smoke formed little moons of its own in the air. "Every day after classes I'd rush home to watch my brothers in the fields, with all the ranch hands Dad had hired. These cowpokes—dark, tough, crusty fellows—they spoke a funny language, like they were a race all their own. I understood the words all right, but their accents were strange, like twangs in a rusty old piece of barbed wire. I thought it was cowboy code or something. Years later, I learned they'd all come from Australia and New Zealand or the Basque country in Spain. There's your Myth of the American West shot to hell," Zack said. "My daddy said it was common knowledge that American boys were too lazy anymore to make good cowboys, so they brought these foreigners over, who knew the value of work. So I *had* been right. They *were* a race of their own, though they hadn't all come from the same stock. No matter how I tried, I'd never be one of them. They shared the land they worked and the experience of sailing here from far away. No one else on the planet knew what that was like, not exactly."

He stood and poured us more whiskey.

"Well, of course I never went off and became an educated man like yourself."

I started to raise my hand.

"No no," Zack said. "I admire you, Jon. Really. But I don't feel sorry for myself, either. We're all different, we all choose different paths. It's no big deal. It's not like my daddy stopped loving me. But when I dropped out of school, they drafted my skinny ass and I wound up in the A Shau Valley, north of Laos. This was '69. I experienced it again. The same thing I'd felt around the cowhands, only this time I knew it from the inside. I don't know how to say this, Jon, but there are certain places and things you do—or a combination of the two, I guess—that make a unique impression on a man's mind, and fix that moment forever in his blood."

I thought of Pound's definition of art: an "intellectual and emotional complex in an instant of time."

"No one in this world knows how it feels to slide around in a mud-and-shit storm, fighting for your life with just your hands or a bayonet in that dull awful light from a claymore," Zack said. "No one but my buddies and the men we were trying to kill in those shitty jungles in the hills. They were my enemy then, the VC regulars. But they were there, you see. They understand. We went through something *together* that makes us brothers, 'cause no one else will ever know what it was like."

He ground his cigar with his shoe.

"A big part of me's still in the A Shau," he said. "And I hate the fucking military for putting it there. But the other part of me, the part that came home and married a good woman—it's grateful to the army for taking care of me, for giving me a job I can feed my family with. You know? That's why I protect it so fiercely."

I nodded.

"You were right," he said. He was whispering now. "The Aurora, I mean. I didn't want to say any more about it in front of your kids, but since you know . . . where'd you hear it?"

"Friend of mine," I said. "He has a contact at the Pentagon."

Zack shook his head. "If it ever gets out that I said anything—"

"It won't. Not from me."

His shoulders relaxed. "Thanks."

I asked him what the army would do to stop a leak.

"God knows," Zack said.

"My friend's disappeared," I said. "They wouldn't—?"

He shrugged. "They've got jobs to protect, too."

"What's it do? The Aurora."

"The world turns gray?" He laughed. "You'd better believe it."

Buttery-yellow light fell through the screen door behind us. Piano jazz played on a tinny radio somewhere inside.

"Is this what they call the Dempsey? Is it the same thing?" I asked.

Zack smiled at me. "Let me get some more Old Charter." He turned and walked inside. I strolled into his yard, watching the sky. It was the color of smoked glass. A vivid sheen. I looked for constellations I knew. Leo, with its scythelike head. The Dipper. Delphinus.

For a moment, I thought I could smell the rotten peaches from our little West Texas alley. My father's aftershave. I was a boy again, alert for shooting stars and scrabbling toads, seeking the warmth of my daddy's chest, the fine rumble of his deep, slow voice. . . .

Beth screamed. I ran to the door. Zack had collapsed on the red kitchen tiles. His arms splayed beneath the table. Beth knelt at his feet; they twitched like giant needles on a steam gauge. In the dining-room doorway, Scott shook. Dana stared at her brother. Inside, I dropped to the floor and felt for Zack's heart.

This wasn't the goddam flu.

"Zack, Zack, honey," Beth whispered.

Gently, I moved her aside, slipped my hand beneath Zack's head and steadied myself to lift him. I gasped.

The back of his head wasn't there. His skin was a soiled wet rag full of lumps. I felt as though I'd slit an old, small watermelon.

"Jon?" Beth looked at me, wild.

"Beth, his skull is . . . Peg, call an ambulance. Tell them to hurry."

Beth didn't blink. "Jon?" she said again.

Peg dialed the phone. I was afraid to move my hand; Zack's flesh might come away too.

Scott groaned. He hit the wall in rhythmic bursts. Dana hugged him.

"Jon?" Beth said.

Zack opened his eyes. He smiled. "Jon," he said. He said, "Hey."

Scott stumbled like a marionette on knotted strings. Tears blurred his eyes; he couldn't see his steps in the dark. Dana walked ahead of us, waving her arms, explaining to the night, "His head. His head."

Peg had stayed with Beth and Midge to wait for the ambulance. I wanted to get the kids out of the house. When I'd let Zack go, his skin stuck to my palm like chewing gum. I had to peel it loose. Four times I washed my hands in the kitchen sink, using a bottle of Joy.

I needed air. "Meet you downtown by the post office," I'd whispered to Peg, and hurried the children outside. Tilton was dead this time of night. Vague shadows dithered across drawn curtains. Somewhere, the sound of breaking glass, barking dogs. Tires squealed on the highway heading east out of town.

A kid had left a bat in a softball field, near the missing home plate. Streetlights flickered, the color of milk.

A dull glow lighted yellow grass near a rhododendron garden. The park man was stoking his fire. He looked up when he heard us. Scott froze. He wiped his eyes. "That's him," he said. He reached for my arm.

I said, "What do you mean?"

The park man rose. His hair was loose and wavy, his sweater all-the-way buttoned, his jacket pulled tight. Its black wool collar looked fuzzy in the firelight and brushed his beard in the breeze. He'd made a bed of his raincoat in the dirt.

"The man from my dream," Scott said. "The furry one. That's him." His hands trembled.

The man raised his right arm. He pointed at Scott.

I nudged the children away from him, toward the street.

"Me too," the man said. He stared at Scott.

"What do you want from me?" Scott yelled.

Dana whimpered. "Is he a ghost?" she said.

I gripped her shoulder. "No, honey. Keep moving."

"Me too," the man said.

I scowled at him as if to scare him off. His fire crackled, sending bright orange stars into the trees.

"Me. *Me!* Me too."

We ran to the sidewalk and turned for the post office. Scott watched the man, who continued to point at him, until we were well out of sight of the park.

MY FATHER DIED in Dallas on Valentine's Day. Heart failure, the doctors said. I questioned the head physician on the phone: a man enters a retirement home with a broken ankle, and leaves on a stretcher? How is that possible? What kind of bonehead operation are you running out there?

But I knew the doctors weren't at fault. I'd heard the fatigue in my father's talk whenever he'd called. Camelot had long been kaput, the oil boom was over. My mother wasn't my mother anymore. Dad had capped his well the day he'd left his house.

I booked a flight to Texas. My work could coast just now. An art dealer in New York had managed to secure for me, on loan from several private collections, a dozen Joseph Cornell pieces: shadow boxes filled with star charts, marbles, fauns, stereopticon shots, pale lunar bubbles.

While Tommie drove me to the airport, I repeated my installation instructions for her and reminded her to file the insurance forms. As usual, she didn't quite listen. She said her home life was dull as dust. She'd cut her hair so her husband would pay more attention to her. "He hardly ever looks at me," she said. "If he's watching sports on television or something I could understand it. I like a man who enjoys his sports. But Wade just stares at the walls and eats on his days off. Something wrong with a man who doesn't like sports."

"Right," I said. Conjugal bliss in the great state of Nevada.

The night before, Scott had promised he'd look after Peg. Each morning she joined Beth Heron in a hospital vigil for Zack, who remained in critical condition, diagnosis unknown.

"I don't want you to worry about stuff," Scott told me. "I can handle things here."

I shook his hand. "I know you can," I said. Neither of us mentioned the park man. For now, Zack and Dad claimed our thoughts. "I have faith in you, son."

This afternoon two irritable old men, bound to their wheelchairs with thick silk straps, sit in the Parkview Manor lobby in front of the big-screen TV. An old cop movie in black and white: leering killers, screaming women. The actors' faces, flattened and pale against the lime-green wall behind the screen, remind me of old photographs I've seen in the memory books here, on nightstands beside the beds.

A slow ceiling fan swirls dust motes across the lobby floor. Flies light on the old men's cotton sleeves. They're wearing yellow pajamas—standard Parkview dress—and leather slippers. They don't like each other: I can see that. Both are new arrivals here, never met before today, but while the movie hums at high volume these two guys are giving each other the glare. My mother's asleep; I've stepped into the lobby to stretch my legs, to get a Coke from the patio machine out front. As I'm sorting dimes I hear one old bird rasp at the other, "You son of a bitch," and suddenly they're both throwing punches. The rubber wheels of their chairs squeal against each other and scuff the red tile floor. These fellows are too weak to really hurt each other, but the nurses panic and glide them toward separate corners of the room. "Mr. Davis! Mr. Edwards!" shouts one of the nurses' aides. On the television screen, a masked burglar jimmies a window.

Good for you, I think, watching the old men grimace and cough. Don't let the fire go out, the way my father did. (I swear I've heard—late at night, when only Nurse Simpson's on duty,

Nurse Simpson, who lets me stay if Mom's had a hard evening
—I swear I've heard the sounds of sexual pleasure, whether from
memory—a murmuring in sleep—or actual contact, I can't tell.)

I go to check on Mother. She's awake now, lying in bed,
clutching her box of Kleenex. She's nearly blind; if she pats
around the sheet and can't find her Kleenex she cries. Her hands
are tiny and clawlike, tight with arthritis. Sometimes, to exercise
or just to pass the hours, she rolls and unrolls a ball of blue yarn.

I ask her if she wants some apple juice.

"Yes," she says.

I turn the crank at the end of the bed to raise her up; hold
the cup, guide the straw into her mouth. Her teeth are gone.

"You tell him to talk to me," she says.

"Who?" I ask.

"Stubborn old man." She waves at a chair by the wall. "He's
been sitting there all afternoon reading that damn paper and he
won't talk to me." Her voice cracks. "Where's your whore today,
old man? Off with someone else?"

I stroke the papery skin of her arms, offer more juice. She
doesn't even know Dad's gone. I'm just a friendly stranger.

Sunlight spreads, first bright then pale, through her peach-
colored curtains. An air-conditioning vent above her bed flutters
a poster taped loosely to the wall. Yesterday a Methodist church
group, on their regular visit, left these posters in all the rooms: a
little girl hugging a kitten. The caption reads, "I Know I'm
Special—God Don't Make No Junk."

"Can I get you something else, Mom?"

"French fries."

"All that grease?"

"Get me some goddam French fries!"

I don't know how she chews the silly things with just her
gums, but she does. "All right," I say. "I'll be back."

In my rented Toyota I drive a few blocks to a Burger King.
The streets here on Dallas's west side are lined with sexy new
cigarette ads—enormous, rolling breasts filling billboards. I lift my

foot off the gas pedal and coast in my lane, staring, lonely for Peg, at the huge women floating like helium balloons over the start-stop traffic. Tears blur the dashboard lights.

My father didn't want to be buried in the desert or in the city; he chose the Gulf Coast of Texas, where in his prime he'd discovered tons of oil. Years ago he'd bought plots for Mom and himself in a small cemetery overlooking steaming white refinery spires in the bay. Early one morning, on a red-eye special out of Dallas's Love Field, I accompanied his body to Houston.

At night near the cemetery, foghorns called across the water. Orange flames cast purple shadows on tall blue thunderheads rolling over the coast. Sulfur and carbon singed the air. The ground was moist; my shoes were caked with twigs and mud. Standing near the grave I imagined my father sinking deeper into the earth, falling away with his hopes and fears into the loam and shale and rocks he'd pumped dry all his life: the jelly of the centuries, packed tightly into fissures. Tankers sailed into the gulf. *Vaya con Dios,* Dad. Welcome home.

In folktales a father's death often frees a son to live his own life, fully, for the first time.

I sat in my hotel room, crying, drinking scotch until I couldn't stand up.

I phoned my sister in Atlanta, whose husband and kids had the flu. She said she wished she could've been here with me. (I knew she wouldn't come; she and Dad were never close.) I phoned home. Scottie answered.

"Everything all right?" I asked.

"Fine. Mr. Heron's the same. Mom spends a lot of time at the hospital."

"You're looking after Dana okay?"

"Yep."

"What about you, pal? Any bad dreams?"

He coughed. "Some. Dad?"

"Yes?"

"How does it feel not to have a father?"

I poured myself another drink. The room began to spin. The old man wasn't here anymore to tell me to watch my step. His generation was slowly blowing away. People *my age* were in charge now. My God. "Funny," was all I could mumble into the phone.

Scott said I should probably get some sleep. I laughed. "Yessir," I said, scotch and love burning my brain.

"Hang in there, Dad," he said.

Along with a copy of his will and his investment information, my father had left a few photos in his desk drawer. The gray Impala. The black Mustang he'd bought in '64. The old blue Caprice. A frugal man, he kept all his cars until they rotted. Spark plugs, pistons, oily fan belts littered my childhood lawns.

Somehow he'd lost all his pictures of the wreckers with their heavy iron chains that sooner or later always came and towed these splendid autos out of our lives.

Week's end, in Dallas. The retirement home is quiet. Water trickles inside a brown plastic air conditioner wedged into a window by the main desk in the lobby. The nurses play Hearts or Spades.

Mom's been sleeping. Now she blinks her eyes. "Where've you been?" she says, a hint of recognition in her voice.

"I'm here, Mom." I fluff her pillows. She asks me to read her the paper. I can't find one.

"I need a story," she says. "Expect me to lie here all day, just worrying and waiting for that old oil field woman to show, with nothing else on my mind—"

"Okay," I say. "I've got a story, Mom."

"What's it about?"

I try to remember bedtime tales I used to tell the kids. Nothing comes to mind. I shouldn't have spoken so soon. "I think it's about . . ." On her wall the poster flutters, the little girl hugging the kitten. I feel dumb that this gooey scene can move me, but it does. I'm raw with emotion for Dad. "I think it's about redemption."

Mom licks her dry lips. "I don't like religious stories."

"No no, this isn't like that." I get her a glass of water. "This one's about a woman in an oil field, but she was a good woman, Mom, not like the ladies you've heard of."

"A good woman?"

"A *very* good woman. Men came to her—"

"*Bet* they did."

"—and she'd turn them away. Said, 'You've got a wife and kids back home. Don't mess with that.'"

"Who *is* this woman?"

"She'd bring folks together again, folks who'd lied to each other and said hurtful things. Told the ladies at home, 'Your man's brave in the fields, works hard all day, so don't you bad-mouth him for not being around.' And she'd tell the men stories of their women, how they sacrificed raising the children, but how nice and bright they all were, how much they all missed him, and the men'd smile and watch oil gush out of the ground—"

"Damned old oil, ruined *everybody's* life . . ." Mom says.

"No, Mom, the oil was good. Built factories and schools. . . . this lady I'm telling you about, the Mayberry Woman they called her—"

"Mayberry? That ain't the story."

"It is, Mom."

"She was a bad woman. Awful old bitch."

"No, she was good. Listen. *Listen.* She used to bathe in oil, in a solid-gold tub with these lion-claw feet made of brass, see? She rubbed thick crude on her arms like she was lathering in riches. Then she bottled up her fortune and shared it with everyone in Texas, men and women both."

Mom's breathing evenly now. Her hands lie still on her tissues.

"See, it's all right, Mom," I say. "It's always been all right, if you remember it this way."

The parking lot fills with noise. A Methodist youth group—eight ten-year-old girls with their mothers—bursts inside, giggling and shouting. The girls are carrying bunny rabbits. They dump the rabbits into the laps of three or four women in wheelchairs. "Is it Easter?" a deaf old woman asks.

"No," the tallest mother says. She seems to be in charge. "We thought you'd like to pet them."

"Is it Christmas?"

Mr. Edwards glares at the bunnies as though he'd like to kill them.

I offer to wheel Mom into the lobby so she can feel the soft fur, but she doesn't want to. She smells like the sweet roll she had for breakfast.

Her eyes cloud up, like marbles. Her mind's about to gallop off to the East Texas fields. She sleeps for a while. When she wakes she tries to convince me that the Mayberry Woman has murdered Dad and buried him here at the home. "On the patio. By the Coke machine," she says.

"Would you like Nurse Simpson to check for you?"

"Bitch won't tell me."

"Why not?"

"She was sleeping with him too."

"Nurse Simpson? I don't think she was Dad's type."

"Don't kid yourself," Mom says. "They're all his type."

She pounds around on the sheet for her Kleenex. When I give her the box she won't let go of my hand. The room's grown dark. Outside, sparrows squabble with a blue jay for space in a bare plum tree.

"I should've killed him myself," Mom says.

Her hand begins to tremble in mine. "Shhh," I say.

"Don't shush me, old man. Just get out of this house."

She tries to shove me away. "She's out there," she whispers, knotting the tissues in her hands. "She's out there waiting for me."

I say, "I know, Mom. But we don't have to go to her just yet." I smooth her hair and tell her again my story of the woman in the oil field.

In my early twenties, before I met Peg, I attracted women by acting depressed. I really *was* depressed most of the time—reasons having to do with sex and money and ambition, and the impossibility of sustaining any sort of pleasure. I went to movies alone and sat in restaurants reading books. The stories I read in public seemed to stay with me longer than pieces I read at home.

A number of women found my black moods sexy; I used misery to my advantage until it began to feel disingenuous and boring, even to me. After that, I accepted my depression as a constant state of mind, went about my business, and was, on the whole, a much happier person.

On the flight home from Dallas, my weary sighs charmed the pretty young stewardess. She checked on me every few minutes, topped my plastic cup with Pinot Noir. Her attention embarrassed me but made for a wonderfully pleasant flight.

In my grief for my father—and again, and always, for my mother—I felt a kind of inner collapse. When I was a kid, the cardboard skeleton I hung on the front door at Halloween had copper rivets in its elbows, shoulders, hips, and knees. The rivets were loose so the joints could bend, but tight enough to hold the limbs at threatening angles. In time, the cardboard thinned; the rivets couldn't sustain active arms and legs. The skeleton hung limp, more sorry than scary. That was me after Texas.

I wished Peg and I could take some time alone, away from the kids. I remembered only a couple of occasions when we'd managed to get away. Once, in Oregon, we took a picnic into the Coast Range foothills, just the two of us. The children were staying with friends. That day, snow patches lingered in the mountains' shadows, lupine blazed in fields. Mimulus, Indian paintbrush . . . glorious in their brief season. I felt a happiness close to hilarity, breathing the cool, polleny air, holding Peg's hand as we scrambled up moist granite ridges trimmed with daffodils and watery yellow light.

Leaves, pale as soft-boiled eggs, twinkled all around us. The trees seemed thin and naked in the world. We danced in the woods until we floated. I needed that feeling again. I wanted to waltz with Peg in the air, here on the blinking wing of the plane.

22

IN MY ABSENCE Peg had been arrested. She'd spent all of one morning with Beth Heron in Zack's room at the hospital; that day after lunch she'd hiked into the foothills for yellow wildflowers, to make me a welcome-home bouquet. In a small meadow east of town she'd run across a flat stone marker wrapped in weeds: THIS SITE WILL REMAIN DANGEROUS FOR 50,000 YEARS. She dropped her flowers and ran.

That evening she took Beth a turkey sandwich and some fresh tomato soup and the two women ate together in a waiting room at the hospital. At ten a doctor told Beth that Zack had passed away in his sleep. No pain. Beth was too stunned to speak. Peg pressed the young man for a cause. Zack's work station at Mesa Bend was near an exposed exhaust pipe for a plutonium-processing furnace, he said. Every day for seven months Zack had stood with his back to the pipe, which—he pulled Peg aside, out of Beth's hearing—hard-boiled his brain.

Beth, shaking, accepted a second helping of Peg's soup, along with a mild sedative. Peg left her with Midge, put the kids to bed, then drove to Mesa Bend, a vast steel compound north of town surrounded by dry riverbeds and salt-white caliche cliffs. All night she danced ("slow spins and arcs") beneath an orange quarter-moon—"gestures of purification," she said. When the morning shift arrived they found her there. She told anyone who'd listen, including the press, what the doctors had said about Zack. She'd made a paper sign and taped it to the chain-link fence: "Confess."

The police, who'd merely warned her when she'd built the "Cleanup Hut," hit her this time with trespassing and disturbing the peace.

Heavy men dragged her to a car. She screamed Zack's name at a quiet crowd of workers near the fence.

Beth and Midge made bail just as my plane arrived from Dallas.

Later, in our trailer, she assured me she was fine. Scott didn't say anything. He twitched and touched the wall. Dana kept her cool.

Peg rejected my suggestion that she and her friends perform in the gym. "Why not?" I said. We'd gone to bed after a light supper. "After this morning's publicity you're guaranteed a full house, honey—and it's legal."

She said theaters—even our musty gym—were much too sanitary. The audience felt comfortable in its soft, assigned seats; it knew the role it was supposed to play, and was sealed from the action onstage. A sanctioned performance wouldn't stir people. The only art that matters now is activist art, she said, work that passionately engages our dear, dying planet. The "Cleanup Hut" was a start, but bolder tactics were in order.

I told her to please stay home, to care for herself and the baby.

"A friend of ours was just murdered," she whispered.

"Peggy—"

"The poison is *real*, Jon. We're not going to send it away with symbols or pretty pictures. Metaphor's as deadly as cancer."

"All right, but—"

"Time to clean the mess." She switched off the lamp.

I thought, What happened to the dedicated mother who wrote, *I'd have pushed the rest of my days to get Scottie born?* "Peg," I said. "Let's talk about this."

Moonlight moved, dim as memory, through our room.

"We just did, sweetheart. I'm tired now. Really."

Welcome home.

A line in the sand, Peg called it. A wall of women. Their numbers had grown.

On the eastern lip of the Site, tents, wooden shelters, and outhouses began to appear. The women planted vegetables, after testing the safety and richness of the soil, built storage huts, workshops, painting and ceramics studios.

"For most men, politics is a matter of ideology," Peg told me. "For women it's the body. We're trained since we're young to use our physical selves. Naturally it's our asses, and not just our thoughts, we lay on the line."

The county refused to issue the women an occupancy permit; the decision was being appealed. Peg never stayed the night, but spent long hours with her friends.

Bright, hand-painted murals hung on poles in staggered rows along the Test Site's rim: missiles, screaming babies. Peg insisted on positive imagery as well. "If we can't imagine a better world, it'll never come to pass," she said.

The women ate from clay plates they'd made. They sang every night. Peg taught them sweeping new movements. At dusk I glimpsed them against the purple horizon, swirling like scarves. Half women, half swans.

Sometimes I brought them groceries, batteries, soap. The group's tone had changed, and not for the better. Most of the newcomers were protest veterans, media-savvy, tough and uncompromising. Despite my ties to Peg, a few of them accused me of being a cop or a spy from the DOE.

One night Scottie and I climbed the hill with a couple of sacks. The moon was starting to rise—a pocked sliver like a cantaloupe peel. We were gritty with dust. Whispers in the dark. "Peg?" I said.

A tight circle of women stopped us halfway up. Sweaty and tall, they smelled of sage. The power of the body again. Oil fields and Love Nests.

Lysistratas in the hills.

The corn and squash we'd brought, still moist from their bins in the store, fell through the wet bottoms of our sacks.

"Who let them in here?" one woman said.

"What's your business? Who are you?"

Scott began to stutter and touch the sandy rocks. The women fell back in disgust.

"It's all right, son," I said. "Help me with these, okay?" I bent to retrieve the food, silver now in the lunar light.

A few minutes later, Peg trotted down the hill. "This is my boy!" she told her companions. She wrapped him in her arms.

"He's a man," one of the women, a broad-shouldered redhead, answered. "Besides, he's wacko or something. Look at him."

Peg rose and slapped her, hard, across the face. "This is my child," she said. "My child is not wacko."

The woman spat at Peg's feet, glanced at me, then away. "Peggy, my love." She rubbed her jaw. "If you weren't pregnant—" She shook her head, then stalked off, followed by the other women.

"Nice lady," I said when they were all out of earshot. "Strict testosterone diet?"

"Please, Jon. It's hard work up here. People get tense."

"That's no excuse."

She glanced at me sharply. Scottie hummed against her chest. I told him, "Let's go. We'll wait for your mother at home."

In the next few days, according to Peg, a solemn debate split the camp. The lesbians in the group voted to banish all men, but that rule didn't last. Susie, the big Navajo woman, missed her children, both of whom were boys. Peg said some of the straights complained about "extremists" ruining the women's reputation. "The press is calling us all dykes, and that draws attention from our purpose here," one said. "Make love to whoever you want, okay, but let's not be so vocal about it."

This sent the lesbians into an uproar. Nuclear protests were the province of radical feminism, they said; men built the bombs and it was going to take women to destroy them.

Meanwhile each night, our phone rang nonstop. "Damn cunts!" the callers said.

Or: "Who wears the pants over there? She's *your* wife."

"They're all up there naked, I'll bet, flaunting their perversions in front of God and *everybody!*"

"Someone ought to shoot 'em, then you."

"Hit the road, Jack, and take those bitches with you."

One evening while Peg was chairing an emergency caucus at the camp and I was cleaning the trailer, I noticed her purple notebook in a closet. A paper clip marked a page near the end. She'd added an entry:

> *The other night I read a book by a member of IMRO, an organization-for-change around the turn of the century: "The revolutionary is something of an ascetic who has given up the idea of enjoyment and personal happiness. Not one of us will marry and settle down." Well. A bit overzealous. Personal happiness is one of the things my sisters and I are fighting for, but everyone has to be able to experience it or there's no joy at all.*

My sisters? I thought. What's wrong with the *family?* I felt abandoned, and began to resent the women who'd claimed my wife.

The phone rang, startling me. The kids were in bed. When I answered, I heard only a click and mechanical whine. Wind whipped dry cactus needles against our Plexiglas windows. Zack's face muscled its way into my mind. I don't know why. A jet boomed overhead. Filled with angry energy, I placed Peg's notebook back in the closet, grabbed a sponge and a rag.

I crawled around the heater vents, scrubbed beneath the

stove's greasy eyes. I felt compelled to free the trailer of impurities, especially those I couldn't see. Microbes and amoebae; hair; dead skin cells; invisible glue and ink from book bindings, newsprint, pamphlets; oxidized aluminum particles flaking off the window frames. I once read that aluminum can heal itself, the way human flesh grows in over a cut.

By the time I'd exhausted myself I was feverish and sore.

Peg got in at two. She stared at the Ajax, Pine Sol, rags, and rubbing alcohol on the white kitchen table, the filthy knees of my jeans.

"Spring-clean," I said. "How are you?"

"Don't ask." She slumped into a chair. "Six hours. But we finally reached a compromise."

Scott stirred at the sound of her voice. He slipped out of bed, poured himself some milk, and sat with us.

"And?" I said.

She glanced at our son. "I fought this, Jon. I really did."

I wiped the sweat from my face. "Fought what?"

"The camp's new rules. Male children ten and under are kosher. Older than that, well, we won't allow them in."

"Why ten?" I said.

"The general feeling was that boys ten and over are capable of rape. They can't be trusted." Before I could say anything, she added, "These women, they're good people, Jon, it's just that—"

"Damn it, Peg, that's nuts."

She nodded.

I played with the rag in my hands. She'd said our future was her work; now we were barred from her world. She'd urged me to accommodate the public; now *she* was on the edge. "All along, you've said we shouldn't leave unless we find other options," I said quietly. "For the kids' sake. But now I think, no matter what—"

"Jon, I can't hear this. Not tonight. I've got too much—"

"Things are getting out of hand, Peg. It's dangerous."

Scott pounded the table with his head.

"Honey," Peg said. "Oh honey, no no." She reached for his shoulders, looked up at me. "I'll be very careful. I promise."

"That's not what I'm worried about. Your children don't have a mother these days."

"Jon, that's not fair. I'm not going anywhere."

"Are you sure?"

"I swear."

I stared at her until she glanced away. "It seems to me you've already left," I said.

"Me too," Scott said. He swept my rags to the floor. "Hope not hope not hope not."

A legal rep from Mesa Bend asked Beth Heron to donate her husband's brain to the plant. They wanted to double-check the hospital, conduct their own autopsy, adjust their safety procedures. In her grief and confusion she agreed. Soon thereafter the brain disappeared. She never saw or heard from the man again. Mesa Bend denied it had ever sent a representative to her house.

She sought damages, worker's comp, anything. She hired a Vegas lawyer. He told her, "Negligence charges rarely stick in cases like this. The Supreme Court nearly always sides with the DOE. They've made it virtually impossible to collect civil penalties under federal law."

Beth told him to please do the best he could.

Each day on my way to work I brought her doughnuts and grapefruit. Zack's funeral had been delayed because of the missing brain. Beth was starting to fray; my morning gestures seemed to help.

Today, as I left her house, thunderheads flared in the east. Lightning scored the hills; static bristled through my radio. The DJ followed Merle Haggard with a test of the Emergency Broadcast System. He said this was the last time the station would ever use the EBS. The government was phasing it out—another relic in the pale light of the post–Cold War.

The high whine pierced my speakers. I remembered lying in

bed at night when I was a boy, playing the radio low. Cold green winter moonlight filled the window; my father's cigar smoke hung in the rooms. Half asleep, I'd hear the test-scree and the tiny bells on Mama's slippers as she paced the kitchen floor, worrying, waiting for my sister to return from a date.

I'd sit in the dark, propped against my headboard, listening (the creaking, the wind in the trees and the bells, the manic emergency scream), convinced that if I held my awareness of the night, I controlled the house and everyone in it. As long as I stayed awake my family would be safe. No missiles would get us.

And they didn't. Time did. And illness.

Only a test.

I turned the radio off.

"Miss Sunshine Unit" posters plastered the gym's outer walls. Last weekend, during an unusually warm late-winter spell, Tilton had celebrated the high school's football championship along with its annual teen beauty contest, held in Cougar Stadium. Dana, still enamored of high fashion, insisted we go.

"Sunshine Unit," we learned, is a nickname for strontium 90.

In the stadium, Peg drew stares. She was a notorious woman since her arrest.

"Hey, it's Hanoi Jane!" someone shouted from the bleachers behind us.

Peg ignored the comments. The bikini competition began. There were no black or Hispanic contestants. Where did their families live? How could they vanish in a place as small as Tilton?

The show's host reminded us that the swimsuit was named for the tiny atoll where H-bombs were tested; like the weapon itself, he said, the suit was "revealing and powerful."

The new Miss Unit wore her bikini at the crowning. The host slipped a silver tiara onto her head and pinned a brooch to her strapless top. He sang of the "blinding flash of her beauty."

This year's "Megaton Honey" was Jennifer Gordon, a seventeen-year-old senior cheerleader at Tilton High. Scott said he'd met her once in the hall, and she was a snob.

"Little Miss Big Bang," Peg said. "*I* get nabbed for a dance of conscience. This little twit's hailed for teasing old libidos. Do you think she's pretty?"

I said, "In a high school sort of way."

The crowd cheered and stamped its feet as the football team escorted Miss Unit to her throne.

Now, a week later, Tilton had lost its good spirits. The *Examiner* was thick with gloomy forecasts of further arms reductions, defense layoffs. A possible Democratic White House.

I told Chick to tear down the beauty pageant posters. All morning I planned a new show: middle-class fashions of the fifties. Back then, heavy wool suits and wide-brimmed bowler hats were thought to protect average citizens from fallout.

What were women supposed to wear? Did Civil Defense issue any guidelines? I made a note to check.

No word from Harper. His friends at the paper were baffled.

At noon I walked to Grandma's Bakery for some pastry. One of my colleagues from the Steering Committee at Dana's school was leaving as I opened the door. She didn't acknowledge me. In recent meetings I'd objected to the "history" our kids had been forced to learn. In class, Dana's teacher taught the Trinity test and V-J Day, but never mentioned Hiroshima. She'd used the term "Yellow Peril" to describe the Japanese. The mothers didn't see a problem: the teacher was "telling the truth."

At break, over cookies and punch, they whispered Peggy's name.

As I sat in the bakery sipping coffee I saw a couple of camp women enter the laundromat down the street. Daily, the paper ran editorials damning their "loopy politics," letters calling them "pigs," "jiggling bimbos." Readers worried about a tax hike; extra cops had been hired to keep the peace.

I headed back to work, past the laundromat. The sky smelled of showers ready to burst. Inside, by the dryers, the campers had stripped to their panties and bras and were washing the clothes off their backs. An old woman stared at the hair on their legs.

They laughed at her discomfort. God knows I wasn't a Tilton booster, but the women's growing rudeness—the newcomers' influence—angered me too.

Campers crowded the supermarket, the sidewalks, and the park. A few early rhododendrons were starting to bloom. I saw a straw of smoke through slick, sharp leaves. The furry man. I paused for a moment, watching the women, then followed a pair of them in T-shirts, shorts, and boots down a well-pruned flower trail.

He was there, still. Scottie's dream. Ghostly and real all at once, like my mother's oil field woman. In the afternoon light, tending his fire, he didn't look so frightening. Smothered in his heavy coat, he was clearly old and frail. Hungry. Soft whiskers dusted his chin.

A perfectly ordinary lost soul.

He fed a cotton glove to the flames.

"Hello," I said.

He smiled as if he knew me. Newspapers stirred like sleeping cats around the open toes of his shoes.

Now that I was here, what did I want from him? Campers passed us, leaving town. They carried bedrolls, toilet paper, boom boxes. The man watched them, delighted, and seemed to forget I was there. "Do you know my son?" I asked him, blushing, feeling stupid.

He scratched his crotch.

In the pile of papers I spotted Zack's face. His obituary.

A pang in my chest.

The old man watched my eyes. "Me too," he said—a voice strangled with phlegm. With a scabbed finger he tapped the top of the page. He reeked of urine and shit. "Me too."

"You too *what*?" I said. "What do you mean?"

"Me too." He rose, lowered his coat. The back of his head was soft, spattered with old red sores. Splotchy bruises.

What was he telling me?

"Mesa Bend?" I said.

He didn't respond.

Was he damaged like Zack?

He returned to his fire. I didn't know what to say. "Can I bring you anything? A blanket? Some food?"

He tossed Zack's picture into the blaze.

"Listen, I'll come back later with some bread or something, all right?"

"Me too," he whispered.

Thunder broke above the mountains. The man looked up. Fat drops of water hit and hissed in his fire.

The hospital finally released Zack's body for a proper burial. His brain was still gone.

The service was brief. Zack's old buddies from Mesa Bend nodded at Beth from a distance, over the grave. I wondered how many of them had made threatening calls to our trailer.

I held Beth's hand. Together we watched the Sawmill Mountains shiver in morning heat. In the brutal sunlight the world seemed made of color dots, like a late Seurat or a newspaper ad.

I missed Zack's gentle voice, his sudden laugh, his heavy, swaggering amiability.

I could count on one hand the number of friends I'd made in Tilton. I could lose three fingers and still be right.

Beth's lawyer had urged her to drop her case. He'd found numerous safety violations at the plant, but no one to pin them on. "The manager says he was following orders from the Bickwell Corporation, which has a sizable interest here; Bickwell claims it was acting on behalf of the DOE. Believe me, Ms. Heron, the Justice Department won't blow the whistle on a sister agency. You'll drop a bundle of cash and end up nowhere."

Her day-care income barely covered her house payments. Mesa Bend claimed she owed *it* two thousand dollars: she'd miscalculated Zack's sick leave time. Peg and I lent her cash for the lawyer.

"I just feel so betrayed," she sobbed one night. "We trusted them and they killed poor Zack. If that's not a *crime*, what is it?"

"It's bad public policy," her lawyer said. "But we can't prosecute anyone for it."

The day of the funeral, the dark soil of the cemetery was nearly the color of old motor oil; I recalled my father, years ago, puttering around our cold garage one night, waving a trouble light, tinkering with our big blue Caprice. The car was out of sorts. My family was not on the move.

Dad blew on his hands for warmth. A greasy auto repair manual lay on the floor, open to a transparent engine reduced to its parts. O-rings and washers. Caps and plugs. Rules and advice, back when the world made sense.

That night I chased the fog of my father's breath round and round his tool bench, but it always sailed out of reach.

Beth pressed my hand. "Forevermore," the preacher said.

Peg whispered, "Sorry, so sorry." Beth hugged her.

The Bickwell Corporation donated a bouquet of roses to the funeral, and afterward, twenty-five dollars to a memorial fund in Zack's name at the plant.

23

"'THE BEAUTY of a proliferated world, which you and your wife have failed to appreciate, Mr. Chase, is that nuclearization of regional conflicts often proves to be locally stabilizing, though future proliferators, especially those blessed with natural invasion corridors, may indeed reappraise and erode the nuclear taboo that has heretofore guaranteed worldwide military hegemony."

General Thompson hadn't spoken to me since my first night in Tilton. I'd forgotten how loud he could be; I held the receiver several inches from my ear, and grew angrier and angrier as he talked.

"Obviously, sources of safety are temporary at best. Satisfaction requires enormous expenditures of manpower and money—and of course it's always the case that any endeavor launched against one cause to the neglect of others risks deterioration of the remaining situations. Adaptive continuity is the key to readiness—it's *the* story of the late twentieth century—cognizant always of the human proclivity for acceleration. Do you follow me?"

"Not at all."

He wondered if he could discuss with me my security check. It seemed there'd been a snag, he said, a "rather troublesome item" on my résumé, a trip to Central America.

So that was the game. I couldn't wait any longer. The trap

195

was about to snap shut on me. "Fine," I said. "But there's something you should know before we go on, General."

"What's that?" he said.

I took a breath. "I quit."

A college deferment kept me from serving in Vietnam, like Harper and Zack, but I *do* have a war story to tell:

One night in the summer of '86, wild dogs and roosters cried in the hills around Ocotal, Nicaragua, a small farm town twelve miles south of Honduras. Their echoes in the matted forests were like muted groans of the dead. The tour bus I'd ridden all day was parked in the lot of a blacked-out hotel, next to a Red Cross ambulance, the only other vehicle in sight. The manager padlocked the gate. He refused to feed us. "Goddam *gueros*," he muttered. He spread small silver room keys on his battered oak desk and told us to go to bed quietly. "You must leave the lights off!" he warned in Spanish. The bus driver told me the enemy was near. He pointed north, past thick, dark coffee groves. "Many contra camps there."

Gunpowder soured the air.

I'd come to Nicaragua to meet its artists, to see the murals they'd made (the great clash of history—machetes and armored tanks), but here, on the front line of the war, the walls they'd painted had shattered.

Boarded windows, empty streets.

A week before, sixteen people had died in the central plaza, in a vicious mortar attack. Our tour guide wasn't supposed to expose us to danger, but we'd kept him on the road all day, asking to visit out-of-the-way villages, and we'd wandered off our itinerary. The driver refused to travel at night in a white bus, easy to spot, so we'd stopped in Ocotal.

From my room I listened to the fierce, lonely hunger of the dogs. It was August, but the air was cold. Mist traced my dirty window. I hadn't showered in a week, but here, as in other towns, hot water and soap had long since disappeared. I stepped into the john, unzipped my jeans. A mortar shell rocked the walls. Another fell in a field nearby. My ears popped. My bladder blazed; I couldn't stop it. I dived behind the toilet, pissing myself, the sink, the floor. I'm going to die holding my dick, I thought.

And: My tax dollars have paid for this.

My single brush with the glories of war.

For this experience—"consorting with the enemy," Thompson called it (our tour had been approved by the Sandinista government)—I was in danger of failing my security check. Months ago, he'd read my résumé; he'd known about the trip all along. Clearly, it was just an excuse to put the squeeze on Peg and to force me to become, as Lynn had put it, "one of them."

"You *can't* quit, goddammit, now listen to me—"

"General, I've learned who my real enemies are," I said on the phone. "I can't wait to leave this hole." This wasn't entirely true; I hated taking my kids on the road again.

"Fine," Thompson said. "You have till the end of the month to clear out of our trailer. Town'll be better off without you."

"*Nothing's* going to leave this town better off. Unless a big wind comes and blows it all away."

He yelled, "It makes me ill to think fine young men die every day to keep the world safe for malcontents like you."

"Me too, General. Me too."

At first, Peg pretended not to hear when I told her what had happened. "As it turns out, we're lucky most of our stuff's still in storage," I said. "Not much packing to do. It seems to me our first priority's a good doctor for you and the baby. What was that obstetrician's name in Houston? When Dana was born?"

"I don't remember," she said quietly. She ran a brush through her hair. "I've got to get back to the camp. There's a strategy session—"

"Peg, listen to me—"

"How could you do this?" she yelled. She threw the brush on the bed. Dana grabbed Scott's hand and led him out of the trailer. "How could you do this without talking to me?"

"I *have* been talking to you. Or I've tried, in the few minutes you're home each day."

"I've been working. It's important—"

"I know that. But so is the family. I can't go on being mother and father both."

"How are we going to pay for a doctor without medical insurance? Have you thought of that?"

"We'll find a way." She stared at me. "We will. I don't know. All I know is, there wasn't time to . . . Our lives are going to hell here, Peg."

She rubbed her eyes. She wouldn't look at me. "I can't think about this now. I have a meeting—"

"Screw the meeting. Talk to me."

"You seem willing and able to do the talking for us both," she said, and bumped past me out the door.

"That's not my choice!" I called after her. "I don't choose to make all the decisions and fix the kids' meals and do everything else by myself!"

She kept walking toward the car and wouldn't turn around. In the yard, Dana tried to touch Scott, but he pulled away. He wouldn't look at me, either.

Buster Keaton stood on a runaway boat in a hurricane. The woman he loved clung to the roof of a washed-out house.

The telephone rang. I paused the VCR. Buster froze.

The kids were asleep. Peg was still at the camp.

Eleven at night.

What would the caller say this time? That Peg was a bitch, a traitor to her nation? I was a fag, a wimp, an ape who had no business raising children?

I almost didn't answer, but on the fifth ring I grabbed the receiver, cleared my throat for a shout.

"Jon? It's Harper."

I stuttered.

"Listen, I gotta make this quick, case your line or my line is tapped. I know you're upset with me 'cause I haven't been in touch—"

"Jesus," I said. "You don't know—"

"Sorry. But Leonard and me, we've been working our butts off."

"Are you—"

"Gotta move fast. We're leaving, Jon. Leaving town. I want to talk to you about it. Tomorrow morning, early, say seven-thirty, I'll call again, tell you what to do. Can you meet us?"

"Sure."

"*Mañana.*"

In a series of clumsy maneuvers, Buster docked the boat, tossed a rope to his love, and held her as the storm beat the trees.

Midnight. The bathroom faucet.

"What is it?" I whispered.

Scottie paced the trailer. He was naked from the waist up. "I had a dream," he said.

"Tell me."

"It was like I'd left my body and gone someplace while I slept." He sat beside me. I held him. "I was in a basement of some sort, a damp, dripping basement with light green walls. I was standing in line with several other people, all wearing long robes. Our feet were bare and the floor was gritty and wet. In front of us there was a conveyor belt with large squares like chunks of coal on it. Somehow I knew that my job was to snap these chunks into smaller chunks, which wasn't easy, and place them back on the belt for the next person in line. Then *he* broke the pieces into even smaller bits. Black dust covered my skin . . . just now, when I woke up, my hands felt dirty. I had to wash them."

"It was a dream, Scott, that's all."

He shook against my chest.

"Was the furry man in it? The guy we saw?"

"No. He's gone."

He *was* gone. Yesterday I'd walked to the park with a blanket, a pillow, and a loaf of bread, but the fire was out.

"I just don't feel him anymore," Scott said.

We stepped outside for air. Peg still wasn't home. I wondered if she was still mad at me, if she was okay. Lately she'd been having pains—severe indigestion, Potts had told her, caused by the baby's weight on her intestines. She feared miscarriage, deformity, Tourette's, but she wouldn't slow down.

Our neighbors' air conditioners rattled, dripped, and clicked. The noises set Scottie off. He began to rock back and forth on the balls of his feet. Dr. Wren had advised me to leave him alone in moments like this, though it was sometimes painful to watch. His spasm would pass. For the most part, I accepted Scottie's tics now. They conformed so well to his body, to his speaking and gestural rhythms.

This was who he was.

His tics disappeared altogether whenever he lost himself in a task, like doing homework or a puzzle. Wren suggested drawing. On clear, peaceful nights—no blasts—Scottie made sketches of the sky, adding his own details:

Peg found the sketches excessive and disturbing, but Wren encouraged them, and their symmetry made me think Scott's *inner* worlds were stable and serene, despite his surface eruptions.

Tonight, stars ducked behind quickly dissipating rain clouds. Tires hissed on distant highways. The camp in the hills was quiet. Scott stopped rocking. We walked for a while, then he slowed down. "Dad? What are we going to do?"

"We're going to find a place where we can all be a family again," I said.

"In Texas?"

"Maybe. Or Oregon?" I watched his face.

He smiled. "Are you sure Mom'll agree?"

"She loves us all, Scottie, and she hates this place just as much as we do. It's just that, right now, she's caught up in something bigger than herself. I know that sounds corny, but it's true."

"We're caught up in it too."

"Yes," I said. "We are."

He was silent for a moment, then he said, "Dad, you remember the night we were out here and you told me to stay?"

"Sure."

He touched my hand briefly. "I'm glad I did."

"Me too, Scott. You know, I'm counting on you to change the baby's diapers."

"No way." He grinned.

"No way? What kind of son are you?" I grabbed the back of his neck and shook him gently. He lifted his arms, as if to steady himself. "Dad?"

"Yes?"

"Are we having an earthquake?"

"Why?" I thought he was joking. He didn't smile.

"Feel it?" he said.

"No."

I didn't move. All around me the desert settled—soft shifts of sand as the temperature cooled. I touched a leathery stump of cactus meat, its reassuring, almost human feel.

Then a tremble, getting bigger. Louder. The trailer door fell open. I turned. My punching bag tugged on its chain.

"Dad, it's up above."

The dinosaur track took a step.

"It's right on top of us!" Scottie yelled.

We ran for the door. A sleek silver streak split the dark, then the sky ignited with color: red, yellow, blue, twisting in liquid veils. A fine, bright mist peppered my skin. My eyes stung. My throat caught fire.

Scottie screamed.

Colors burst like bubbles of soap, then, in the space of a breath, night returned, still and hot.

I felt raw.

"Inside," I coughed, grabbing Scott. "It might come back. Shower. Scrub yourself good. And hurry, so I can too."

Dana, sleepy, wondered what had happened. I told her to stay in bed. While Scott was in the bathroom I looked around the trailer. Something wasn't right.

Schoolbooks. Peggy's shoes. Then I noticed a Cheez-Its box on the table, next to a bowl of fruit. The apples were shiny and green, the bananas spotted brown. The box—which I knew was red—was white.

My gut kicked.

I rushed to the refrigerator and found a bowl of store-bought strawberries I'd cut and washed after dinner.

Dana followed me. "Daddy?"

The bowl was pale yellow with a light blue rim. Clear beads of water glistened on the berries' green stems. Blue shadows filled the rough dimples. In the cold light my own hand looked orange, like a square of cheddar cheese. The berries were drained of all hues.

The bowl slipped from my palms and exploded.

The world turns gray.

I showered, then Scott and Dana and I lay in the dark of the trailer. I figured it was the safest place to be right now, with God knew what outside. I told Scott not to rub his eyes. "Just keep them closed. Sleep if you can."

My own eyes itched—less fiercely as the minutes passed. I got up and leaned against the locked door, alert for sounds in the sky, scared and upset, but drifting now and then, soothed a little by the shower. As I stood there listening to my terrified kids toss and whisper in their beds, I remembered the first time I didn't trust my sight or the world around me—my first awareness of the body's loneliness and chancy survival, though I couldn't have said so then. I was six years old, playing with my cousin Olive in my mother's kitchen. The floor tiles were startlingly red, freshly waxed and smelling of limes, the room was pleasantly hot, dense with the scent of stuffing, buttered potatoes, and dumplings. Mother was slicing ripe tomatoes into a bowl of garden-fresh salad and humming a Broadway show tune. The oven door was open (powerful ripples of heat); inside, a golden turkey leaked juice into a crinkled tinfoil wrapping.

Thanksgiving Day.

A spoon-shaped kitchen clock hung above the stove. 4:03— I remember because I'd just learned to tell time. Olive beat two silver spoons on the floor. Mom—the lovely, lucid mother of my childhood—asked me to make her stop. My cousin was a baby then, with only a few words. I snatched the spoons from her hand. She bawled. "Spoon," I said, holding one in the air. "Spoon." I pointed to the clock. It occurred to me that "spoon" and "clock" might blur in her mind. "Truck," Olive said. "No, clock," I said, but I was confused now too. I looked at the oven, my mother; felt the heat, the vivid red color rising into my eyes. At that instant it hit me: what I saw in the kitchen might not match the truth.

What if I *saw wrong*? What if my words weren't right?

"Mom?" I asked. "What time is it?"

"Can't you see for yourself?"

"Yes, but what time do *you* see?"

She was exasperated, trying to finish dinner. She glanced at the wall and told me, "It's four minutes past four."

"And is the oven door open?" I asked. "And is there a turkey inside?"

Without her I was lost. I remember being certain of that. Her knowledge, her soft, warm flesh. If she was taken from me, I had no shot at survival. I simply couldn't make it.

She wiped her hands on an onion-yellow apron. "Jon," she said, "I don't have time to play. I need to get ready for this evening. Now will you please keep your cousin quiet while I toss this salad?"

I gazed again at the oven, floor, clock, and spoons. Olive's jam-smeared face. Mama's legs. I didn't know if any of it was really there, and Mama never gave me an answer.

Now, without her and my dad, I couldn't afford to be lost. My family depended on me; I had no choice but to trust myself. I had to survive, no matter what, so they could make it as well.

I rubbed Dana's knee through her sheet. "Hang in there, sweetie. Everything's going to be all right."

"Where's Mom? Isn't she coming home?"

"Your mother's fine. We'll all be leaving here soon. Together. Don't you worry about a thing."

I blinked rapidly, trying to make the burning go away. I settled into a chair. After an hour or so I opened my eyes, got up, and walked into the kitchen. The Cheez-Its box was fine. My reds had returned. The sting had left my throat.

Scottie seemed okay.

Whatever the plane—the Dempsey?—had dropped, maybe we'd washed it off in time.

"'SOUTH, straight out Elvis Road," Harper told me on the phone. "Keep driving. We'll find you."

Highway 93 was Tilton's link to Vegas. Each weekend, motels along that route held amateur Elvis impersonator contests.

The road twisted into hills. Out past the Pit Bull Tavern, old Sinclair gas stations (with dinosaurs still on their signs) offered "Pop," "Picnic Supp" and "Regular Un—." Torn from adobe walls in recent high winds, "Fossils for Sale" posters filled soft shale ravines. A billboard arrow pointed nowhere. It was an ad for a reptile farm. Beneath the words, a snake painted sweet-potato red bared its fangs at faded yellow highway stripes.

Rain came like hot falling stars, shattered then swam across my windshield.

On a radio talk show, a caller phoned from Vegas: "Seems to me these women at that camp are paying way too much attention to Creation, and not enough to the Creator, you see what I'm saying? This world, and this is the point I'm making, is just an illusion. Don't really matter what happens to it. The only true world is the Kingdom of Heaven."

"I hear you, friend," said the DJ.

Rain-slicked clay slid down runneled slopes east of the road. Thunder hummed, high and far across the mesas.

I passed a smoked-cabrito joint perched on a cliff in a "Falling Rocks" zone.

At the nearby Kangaroo Courts Motel, twenty or thirty Elvises stood beneath a ripped canvas awning. They were bathed in bad yellow light from the blinkers of a Greyhound bus. They were all fat, and getting wet. "Please release me, let me go," one sang— a false king, far from the land of grace.

Blakean lightning broke the sky.

I drove for an hour before I spotted Harper's Mercury in my rearview. Leonard waved from the passenger seat. I slowed, let them pass, then followed.

They led me to the Road Runner, a wooden motel the color of clabber. Over the years, sand and stiff cactus quills had slashed the walls' thin paint. Rain steam rose off the pink twisted neon buzzing "HBO/Heated Pool" on a sign above the office.

Flash lightning froze the hills around us. Dust fell like sifted flour in the air.

Harper apologized for his long silence, and this morning's elaborate plans, but he and Leonard couldn't take chances, he said. They'd discovered some things the army didn't want them to know. They had to keep the Mercury out of sight.

He was excited, dirty, and furtive. Yellow and unshaven. He walked me to a room that smelled of French fries and catsup. Two single beds, an old coppery mirror so dull it reflected only the bare white ceiling bulb.

"Best brown-water shower in the state," Leonard said. "We've holed up here 'bout a month." He shook a metal box nailed to one of the headboards. "Only problem is, the damn Magic Fingers don't work."

"We're heading out today," Harper told me. "We've done all we can and we figure the army's on our heels, so we've got to make this quick, Jon." He hugged me. "It's good to see you."

"I quit my job," I told him. "We'll be heading out too, soon's we can get our stuff together."

"Good. Good. I wanted to talk to you about that. But first."

He pulled a tiny notebook from his shirt pocket. "Here's the whole shebang. You ready?"

"Shoot."

He smiled through his exhaustion, cleared his throat. I noticed he'd lost a few pounds. "All right. Item: two weeks ago, at an underground nuke test, over ten thousand square feet of the Groom Lake plain collapsed, spilling several trucks and people, one of whom later died, into a sinkhole. The incident wasn't reported, but a DOE guy who's agreed to talk to me off the record says the land here is increasingly unstable.

"This same fellow tells me the Test Site will be contaminated forever. His word. *Forever.*"

He rubbed his neck. "Item: the DOE claims it tried to implement its cleanup plan five years ago, burning leftover weapons parts, but 'radical environmental groups' took them to court, insisting incineration was dangerous. Turns out, these environmental groups were put-up jobs—people *paid* by the DOE. In effect, the government sued itself so it wouldn't have to keep its promise."

While he talked, Leonard poked around the room, packing last-minute stuff: sunglasses, combs, and maps.

Harper licked his fingers, turned a page. "More happy news. In a campaign speech in California last week, the Vice President promised tax relief to defense contractors who're willing to sign trade agreements with foreign industries. So even if the U.S. scales back its own arsenal, there's plenty of testing to be done, readying shipments for the highest bidders overseas. It's never going to end here. Add to that the rumors out of Los Alamos—mini-nukes research, smaller yields for police-action wars, well—" He shook his head.

Leonard splashed water on his face, at the sink.

Harper burned with his narrative. This wasn't the easy, cautious man I'd met months ago. He'd found his way out of Tilton, and he wasn't looking back.

"Here's the kicker," he said. "The Aurora, the Dempsey—

they've got half a dozen names for it. Sightings as far away as Fresno—"

"More than one?" I said.

"Three that we're aware of. Fully operational. I knew it didn't make sense for the Pentagon to cancel its Blackbird program after twenty-eight successful years unless they had a crackerjack follow-up." He tapped his notebook. "Item: Mesa Bend's regular employees account for approximately two thousand six hundred vehicles in its parking lots, daily. We found an average of nine hundred extra cars per week. Personnel surplus. Secret project."

Leonard threw a can of lime-scented Foamy into his bag.

Harper said, "Here's how I see it, okay? Liquid methane engines. Halfway between a rocket and a plane. Those early blasts we heard—they've toned them down, streamlined the baby. Spins on a dime. Travels about mach eight. Leaves a thin smoke trail—"

"Or a colored mist," I said.

Leonard whistled. "You saw it again?" He sat on one of the beds. A faded horse hung in a frame above the nightstand and a lampshade scorched with old cigarette burns.

"Right outside my trailer," I said. "This mist stung like hell and blurred my vision, but I scrubbed it all off."

Harper touched my arm. "No aftereffects? Nothing with the eyes?"

"I'm fine."

"You're lucky. Light dose."

"Reservation people have had total blindness, first-degree burns," Leonard said.

"What the hell is it?"

"Chemical. That's all we know," Harper told me. "We've got a small sample in a film canister—"

"Is that safe?"

"We'll find out."

I tapped Leonard's bag. "So where you going?"

"Chinle, Arizona," he said. He packed his toothbrush. "We'll publish our findings in the paper I own."

"And what'll you say, exactly?"

"Witnesses from the old reservation will testify that the United States Armed Forces are practicing chemical warfare, using them as guinea pigs."

"As far as the world knows, that's abandoned federal land," Harper added. "No one knows the Indians are there."

"Damn government *let* 'em back in," Leonard said.

I stared at him. "The Big Man's gone." I don't know why I told him this.

"He came to warn us. His job is done."

I nodded. "He's probably sleeping in an alley somewhere."

Leonard looked at me. He folded a shirt.

"Jon, we're taking a few of the reservation folks with us to Arizona," Harper said. "You're a witness, too. Why don't you come? What are your plans?"

"First step is to kidnap my wife from that camp if I have to," I said. "Her trial's next week—"

"Trial? What trial?"

"Disturbing the peace."

"She's not contesting that, is she? Is she crazy?"

From another room I heard soft laughter, an old *Gunsmoke* episode. Kitty flirting with Matt.

"She says it's a matter of pride," I said. "I've told her the stakes are much higher than that, that she should pay the fine so we can get the hell out of here."

"Exactly," Harper said. He slipped his notebook into his shirt. "Come with us."

Leonard looked around the room. "We should hit it, Harper. Got everything?"

"Yep. Lock and load."

I asked them what they hoped to accomplish, going public. Who'd hear them in the daily din of overinformation, or be perceptive enough to distinguish their story from tabloid rumors or popular fiction?

"I don't know," Leonard said. "But nothing'll happen, sure enough, we don't try."

Outside, the day was still dark. Pale green neon lined the Road Runner's eaves. A shredded newspaper blew across the road and caught in the raised yellow arms of a cactus.

I shook Harper's hand. "Come to Chinle," he said again. "Do yourself a favor. We can help each other, Jon."

I asked Leonard, "Do you have good baby-doctors in Arizona?"

"We have the best of everything." He smiled.

"We'll find you whatever you need," Harper said. "Us West Texas boys, we got to stick together."

I nodded. "You've got yourself a deal."

He clapped my back. "All right, then. All right." He got in the car. "See you in a few days?"

"We'll get there as soon as we can."

The Mercury backfired once. Leonard waved and they headed south down the road, where Elvis lived forever.

In town, the traffic lights are off. The storm has killed a transformer somewhere. Cars bark at one another.

The sky is black with one clear patch, runny and yellow, like an egg yolk. If I saw these clouds on a canvas, I couldn't say if the painter wanted ecstasy or torment. They're fragmenting now, floating off in wisps, leaving more open space.

I park by the gym. A crowd is marching down the street, the women arm in arm. The men carry guns.

Hatred and purpose fix their faces.

"Jesus," I say aloud, halfway out of my car. The camp.

I fall in beside them. No one says a word. My questions hang in the air.

Maybe Peg's with Potts, I think. Lord, let her be home.

Past the barbershop, the beauty parlor, the bank, a parking lot filled with fat American cars—luxury spit-shined and polished, the arrogance of speed. Shop owners lock their doors and join their friends in the street. A sign in the diner's window says, "Back at Noon." Except for the cars, the town looks like a set for an old Hollywood western. All that's missing is the OK Corral.

A young man dances around me, squints in my face, then points a silver semiautomatic at me. "Dave! Hey, Dave! He's one of 'em!" he shouts. "His woman is the main agitator!"

A man in a brown bowling shirt ("Dave—Triple A League") runs over to examine me. "You sure?" he asks his friend. The young man nods. Dave pulls me to the curb. "Stay out of our fucking way," he warns me. "Hear?"

The guns are lovely in the first break of morning sunlight. Smoky blue barrels. Smooth wooden handles, red as earth.

Where are the cops? I think. Where's the goddam army?

The crowd rounds a corner. I splinter off, toward Lynn's house. He's standing in his open doorway. His uniform coat is unbuttoned. "What's going on?" he says. "A parade?"

"Stop this!" I yell. "Those women are unarmed!"

"You know that for a fact?"

I shove his shoulders, then follow him as he stumbles back inside. The kukri sits in a corner beside him. He looks for it. "Forget it," I say.

"Threats, Jon?"

"Get your people, or the sheriff, but stop this now. Someone's going to be hurt."

He reaches, not for the long knife, but for the open bottle of Wild Turkey on his living-room table. "Let's talk," he says. "Join me?"

"You son of a bitch." I swear I'm going to hit him this time, but I need him. I need him scared. I snatch the bottle from his hands and shatter it against the wall. Beads of whiskey glisten in the air, in sudden sunlight from the window. "Now!" I shout. "Be a hero, Major. Just once. You have the authority to head this off."

"Authority?" He crunches broken glass with his boot, shakes booze off his hands. "What do you know about it? It's not like Patton in the movies. You know, I really *did* try to be your friend, Jon. I tried to help you adjust."

For a moment he seems sad. I don't doubt him. I glance through the window; the last of the crowd is almost out of sight.

"Will you call the cops?" I say softly now. "Will you do something?"

He just stands there, looking betrayed.

I turn and run to catch the mob. Main Street peters out and becomes a narrow dirt road leading into the hills. The crowd constricts.

The campers see us coming. They take up bicycle pumps, ladles, and sticks. When the townsfolk enter their space, the women close ranks around us, pressing in.

For a moment no one stirs. Violence beats like a blood-rush in the air. The women squeeze tighter until we all touch. In our haste, confusion, and anger, we've become strangely, suddenly intimate.

I watch the men's fingers on their pistols.

Mosquitoes brush our faces. A hawk cries. Someone sweeps a fly from his nose; the movement sends a ripple through the crowd. I feel the tense, pulsing heart of the skinny man behind me.

"Witches," a town woman whispers. Her voice is rough and deep.

We catch our breaths and blink.

A hand towel flaps on a clothesline strung between an outhouse and a tool shed. Someone's sewn a tampon onto the towel, painted to resemble a warhead.

"Witches," the woman repeats.

The crowd begins to shift. "Burn 'em," someone growls.

A gap opens in the trembling, sweaty web of women's bodies. Susie steps through, magnificent and tall in a stark purple muumuu. She glares at the gunmen. "What can we do for you?" she says.

A pistol cocks. She doesn't flinch.

"Get the hell out of Tilton."

Susie says, "We'll leave when the testing stops." I see behind her the redheaded woman who threatened Peg the night Scott and I were here, the quiet Vietnamese sales clerk from the 7-Eleven in town.

"You'll leave now."

"Or what?" Susie chides the man.

He jostles forward, raising his pistol. When I reach for his arm, he shouts, "What the fuck," turns, and aims the gun at me. "You want a piece of this, asshole?" he says. "I'll be glad to feed you."

Hesitate, dance. Or rush right in.

There are no neutral corners.

He pokes his face in mine. Brown, broken teeth. Whiskers red as ants.

He grins. Though my jab is quick, time slows for me, the way it did the day I finished Peg's journal in the hospital. My own movements don't seem real.

The man is on his back.

Dempsey didn't like to share the ring. A fast kill, he'd say, then you stand alone.

Hammers click. Time stalls again. At that moment I spot Dana's face.

"Baby!" I call.

A gun goes off downhill. Another shot—a warning—followed by a megaphone shout: "Move apart! Break it up! That's an order, goddammit! I mean now!"

Three jeeps with flashing blue lights brake on the narrow road behind us, spraying us all with gravel. The web loosens. Now there's room to breathe. Someone waves a tiny American flag.

The sheriff, a short-legged man named Boone, tops the hill's crest. "There'll be no trouble here today," he wheezes. He spreads his arms, clearing space.

Whether or not he deserves any credit, I thank Lynn in my mind.

"Arrest these women, Sheriff."

"Hold on now," he says.

"Him too." The bowler fingers me. "Assault and battery. No provocation, no provocation whatso—"

"Dave. Shut up," Boone says. "Now I want you all to get back to town."

"Exactly," Susie says. "Go home like good little families and feed your dogs and kids."

"We got *enough* goddam trash here in Tilton."

"Lesbian Commie cunts!"

"Calm down, calm down," says Boone.

"Go join the fuckin' army, dykes!"

"I *was* in the fuckin' army. Nurse Corps, Da Nang. So shove it up your ass."

The sheriff raises his bullhorn again. "Cool it! No one's getting physical here. Everybody just go home. Nothing's going to happen. I mean it. You hear me? Don't give me any flak."

Deputies stroll among us wielding clubs. They're all chewing gum. I smell Wintergreen and Spearmint when they pass. Shouting continues, but Boone has doused the danger. I bump past angry men—all, it seems, with the fat, jowly face of Ernest Borgnine—and hug my shaking daughter. Slowly, the mob begins to thin.

"This ain't the end of it!" someone shouts. The crowd winds down stony slopes. "We'll be back!"

Dana tells me she's fine. Her skin is pale. She swallows hard, twists her fingers into mine. My knuckles throb, from the punch.

"What are you doing here?" I say. "Where's your mother?"

"After we dropped Scott off at school, she asked me to come with her this morning, just for a while. She wasn't feeling good."

"Stomach pains?"

"Yes. They took her to the hospital. I stayed here to pack her things and—"

"What time? What time did she leave, honey?"

"I don't know—an hour ago? Is she having the baby, Daddy?"

If she is, she's six weeks premature. "Let's go see," I say. "Grab your mother's stuff."

Dana picks up a plastic mesh bag with shoes, books, a couple of skirts. We step carefully down a rocky dirt path.

"Those people were going to hurt us," she says.

"We're safe now."

She watches my face, not her footing. I try to hide my worry.

Come join us, Baby Jess. The place is a bit of a mess right now but we swear we'll clean it up.

I'm late, but I'll be there to greet you. Promise. I wouldn't miss it.

Dana nearly trips. I hold her tight.

It's up to me, I think. Everything's up to me. First stop, Chinle. Yes. Chinle, Arizona. Friends are waiting for us there. Quiet nights and good, clean earth. I try to imagine the place, but it's Oregon I see, the lovely valley where my son was at peace, where sunlight scissored quickly through pines in the mornings, then disappeared in blue strands of mist trickling like snowmelt through the foothills. Fall was always our favorite time of year: the last bright days before six sad months of rain. I got a sweet, lonely feeling in September as though drifting on a lake at the edge of a storm. I could smell the rain from miles away, feel winter's first chilly poke in the chest.

I'll get us there, I think. The land of promise where our children can be happy. Sooner or later I'll get us there, safe and sound.

"After Mama has the baby, can we go to Baskin-Robbins?" Dana asks.

"Sure."

"Scott too?"

"Scott too."

"But not the baby. She's not ready yet, right?"

"Right. I'll buy you an extra cone. The one she would've had."

Dana smiles. We run downhill toward her mother.

The hospital feels deserted—long, empty corridors cooled by round electric fans clamped to the walls. We've beaten the crowd back to town. Sunlight burns the last few clouds from the sky; they vanish like a magician's linked scarves as we pass the big clear windows on our way to the elevators. Glary squares warm the brown tile floors, except in shaded corners.

A daylight moon, small as a baby's thumbprint, hangs in a window behind a workstation near the nursery. A fan rattles papers on the desk. Pills click together in paper cups wobbling in the close, moving air. I smell this morning's rain, mixed with dust and the harsher scents of unguents and salves.

A young nurse emerges from a doorway and is startled to see us. I ask about Peg. "This isn't usually my floor," she answers. "Wait here and I'll find someone who can help you."

Dana sits on a stool by the desk. I pace. Peg's spent so little time at home since we argued, I don't know what her mood has been. I remember one evening in her second trimester with Dana, after a wheezy, throbbing day in which she'd had second thoughts—about the baby, me, virtually the entire planet. I snapped a picture of her in the bath. Dime-sized bubbles of soap wavered and popped on her belly. "It's all over for me," she said when she saw me with the camera. She mourned her lost youth. "From now on, it's chicken broth and buckets of drool."

At that instant, she looked to me more sensual than ever. Radiant and pink, with her short hair slicked back. "Talk to me," I said.

"It's your fault I'm this way."

The flashcube sizzled.

Now Dana's laughing at infants through the double-paned nursery glass. I step into a men's room and run cold water over my hand. My knuckles have started to swell. Back in the hall, I stand with my daughter by the nursery. The plastic cradles are harnessed together with nylon straps; the babies look like a team of sleepy sled dogs.

I hear a squeak of rubber shoes, and turn. A slender middle-aged nurse strides purposefully toward me. Her face is weary and sad. My chest tightens. Something blooms, heavy and dark, in my throat.

I don't want Dana to hear the bad news, but she follows me as I approach the woman.

"Mr. Chase?"

"Yes?"

"Congratulations. You're the father of a little girl." She shakes my good hand. She looks sad even when she smiles.

I feel my face burning. I whoop. So does Dana, but quietly. She's still not sure how Jessie will change her days.

I turn to the nursery.

"She's not there yet," the woman says. "We've got her down in ICU for observations. She's awfully small, weighed only three and a half pounds. We'll want to watch her for a few days, but so far everything checks out fine."

My knees buckle just a bit. I've missed another birth.

"Your wife's in the second room on the right," the nurse says, taking my arm. Her uniform smells of Mercurochrome. "You can see her if you like."

"And the baby?"

"I'll walk you down afterward."

I grab Dana's hand. "Three and a half pounds," she says. "That's like a toaster, isn't it? Dad? Isn't that about what the toaster weighs?"

Peg's propped herself up on a couple of pillows and is staring out the window.

She's been crying.

The sight of her so worn brings tears to *my* eyes. "Peg?"

She turns slowly, then her face colors with excitement and relief. "Oh Jon, I'm so glad you're here," she says. Her voice is thin.

We hug—gingerly; she's still sore. Dana sits on the bed and rubs her mother's feet.

"It's okay," I say. "Why are you crying?"

"She's so small, Jon, she's just a little feather, she—"

I smooth her cheeks with my palms. "She's fine, honey. They're taking good care of her."

"I was up at the camp, I couldn't . . . I didn't know how to reach you—"

"I know."

"She's so helpless and frail."

She'd said the same of Scott and Dana. "You know what she is?" I crouch so she can see the sky behind me. "She's like that moon up there. Weak now, but she'll get stronger, and just you wait—one of these nights, watch out! She'll be everywhere."

Dana laughs. Peg finally smiles. She hugs our girl. "Are you eager to see her?"

"I guess," Dana says. "I don't know what to say to her. I mean, she can't talk or anything, right? Can she hear us?"

"Sure she can," I tell her. "And she's going to look to you for help. Here's what you can say to break the ice. Do you remember the rhyme I used to sing when you were little?"

"No."

It was from T. S. Eliot's *Book of Practical Cats*. I recite it for her again:

> *The Rum Tum Tugger is artful and knowing.*
> *The Rum Tum Tugger doesn't care for a cuddle;*
> *But he'll leap on your lap in the middle of your sewing,*
> *For there's nothing he enjoys like a horrible muddle.*

"Do you think you and your brother can learn that and sing it to your sister? I'll bet she'd like it."

Dana nods. She's wondering just how chummy to get with this toaster-sized new person.

"Let's go see her," I say. I kiss Peggy's cheek. "Back in a minute. You okay?"

"I'm fine, now that you're here. What time is it? Is Scottie—?"

"I'll pick him up at school. We're going to be fine, Peg. All of us."

She presses my throbbing hand. I wince a little, smile. Outside, the moon's still clinging to visibility, though the sunshine's brighter now, and I know we'll always remember its gray-and-white face—the crowning detail—whenever we relate this moment to our friends. An unexpected treasure, we'll say, just as Jessie arrived. Wherever we are, whoever we're with, together we'll raise our arms and point. The moon! In the middle of the day!